SPECIAL MESSAGE TO READERS

THE ULVERSCROFT FOUNDATION
(registered UK charity number 264873)

was established in 1972 to provide funds for research, diagnosis and treatment of eye diseases. Examples of major projects funded by the Ulverscroft Foundation are:-

- The Children's Eye Unit at Moorfields Eye Hospital, London
- The Ulverscroft Children's Eye Unit at Great Ormond Street Hospital for Sick Children
- Funding research into eye diseases and treatment at the Department of Ophthalmology, University of Leicester
- The Ulverscroft Vision Research Group, Institute of Child Health
- Twin operating theatres at the Western Ophthalmic Hospital, London
- The Chair of Ophthalmology at the Royal Australian College of Ophthalmologists

You can help further the work of the Foundation by making a donation or leaving a legacy. Every contribution is gratefully received. If you would like to help support the Foundation or require further information, please contact:

THE ULVERSCROFT FOUNDATION
The Green, Bradgate Road, Anstey
Leicester LE7 7FU, England
Tel: (0116) 236 4325

website: www.foundation.ulverscroft.com

REGAN'S FALL

After the death of their father and the removal of their gentle mother to debtors' prison, Regan and her brother Isaac are left in desperate circumstances. Their only hope is to appeal for aid from an estranged relative at Marram Hall, Lady Arianne, whom neither sibling has ever met. Upon her arrival, Regan encounters the handsome and masterful James Coldwell, the local magistrate, but fears that if she trusts him he will throw her and Isaac out of the house — or worse. Then Lady Arianne attempts to do just that . . .

VALERIE HOLMES

◆

REGAN'S FALL

Complete and Unabridged

LINFORD
Leicester

First published in Great Britain

First Linford Edition
published 2016

A catalogue record for this book is available
from the British Library.

ISBN 978–1–4448–2729–3

Published by
F. A. Thorpe (Publishing)
Anstey, Leicestershire
Set by Words & Graphics Ltd.
Anstey, Leicestershire
Printed and bound in Great Britain by
T. J. International Ltd., Padstow, Cornwall

This book is printed on acid-free paper

1

Regan and Isaac emerged through the old oak and ash trees to gaze upon the magnificent sight that was Marram Hall. To their left, the edge of this vast estate led to sandy grass-covered dunes. Fresh air blew in over the German Ocean. This was a place of beauty, yet wild and unyielding at the same time. The Marram estate stretched out from the grassy sandy cliffs on one side to its vast lands of the beautiful countryside of North Yorkshire. The Hall stood across from the neatly laid lawn and long driveway behind ornate iron gates. Its impressive large rectangular windows looked grand. The Hall was sheltered by woodland on three sides and protected by the might of wealth on all.

Regan swallowed. It was just as her mother had described it to her:

beautiful, yet dangerous.

'Regan, how many times have I told you that Mother would not like this? We should not be here.' Isaac looked at her with critical eyes. 'I know you want to help her, but you have to accept that this could be a time-wasting folly. What if they chase us away? What if they have us thrown in a lock-up for trespass? We don't know them. They could accuse us of anything, and then what would happen to Mother? You have not thought this through!'

'No, perhaps she would not approve — but she is not here, is she? We are. And, Isaac, you agreed to at least try.' Her words sounded harsh even to her own ears as she saw her brother flinch as she spoke them. Now was not the time to soften her resolve. 'Isaac, we agreed. I promise that I will speak to Lady Arianne and make sure that I make a clear plea for Mother's case. I will do this, past wrongs will be righted, and I am sure that they will treat us kindly. Time is a great healer. You have to have faith in the good nature of a woman who lived in fear of her husband. Men can be such brutes, Isaac.' She looked at the young man before her and realised that he was no longer the boy who she had helped raise.

He shook his head, disapproving of her words.

'Not you, but some men.' She knew he did not approve of her speaking in such a bold manner, but she considered herself more understanding of such a situation than he could be. 'If what Mother told us about the lady is correct, and she listens to me, then there may still be hope that time will have mended old wounds and we may yet see a happy reunion. If not, then we are in no worse a mess than we are already in now. They cannot lock us up anywhere. We have done no wrong — they have to abide by the law.'

'They *are* the law, Regan! That house owner is the local magistrate, and you expect to just walk in and see his aunt without introduction. You could be thrown off the doorstep and, if you start to explain, you could be the laughing stock of the North Riding of Yorkshire — or they could cover their wrong-doings and accuse us of profiteering or deception or something!'

'You must hold your nerve now, Isaac, please,' she answered softly in order to calm him. He looked away. Regan was wishing that she could hug her brother and tell him that all would be well, as she had done when he was still a child. He was no longer a boy and she had to treat him like the man he had become. She was determined on the path she had set before her.

'There are always people worse off than us. Don't tempt fate, Regan! If talking does not bring forth a solution, your other option is far worse — if we are caught. We are not thieves, and I will not stand by and allow you to justify your actions of taking what is not ours legally, even if morally we should have a claim. If we are thrown in gaol, transported or hanged, tell me who will help Mother then?' His mouth had set in a stubborn line; he was not for bending on this point.

Regan was momentarily speechless, and yet she knew that her throw-away comment to that effect — that she would take what was theirs — should be conceded. If she withdrew that threat then Isaac would be more prepared to humour her main plan of asking for help. Regan swallowed, trying to cover her moment's doubt.

'Very well. I will try to speak to her, but you are on hand if I need to leave quickly, Isaac,' she snapped back, not wanting to give in to the gnawing doubt that his words spoke a truth. 'I will not lower myself to repossess a thing. I promise.' In fact, the rash threat to take something and sell it had been made in a moment of pique; she had not the courage or inclination to become a thief.

'Yes, but I think we should both go to the Hall. I am your brother. It is not respectable for you to present yourself alone. Please, I must keep you safe, Regan. You should be chaperoned. You do not understand the ways of mon-eyed men. You think you do because you have read some of the new ideas of that Mary woman, but you do not.'

'Mary Wollstonecraft . . . '

'They care nought for the welfare of young maids who have hit hard times. Especially when they should shoulder some of the blame for their fall . . . ' He looked away; anger did not become him, not with her. She wanted to tell him that they would go together, but she wanted to protect him, because Regan realised that she could be in a great deal of trouble if all did not go well and they tried to silence her. They had money and position and she had nothing but the word of a woman she adored who was now in a debtors' cell, on the brink of being sent to an asylum, for she had not taken her situation well. If they did not return with the coin needed to save her, how would they ever prevent her from being labelled a lunatic? She had been strong in mind and body, but her claims were seen as madness and flights of fancy. Only they, the owners of this grand house, could give the credence to her mother's claims, if the lady would just speak out and tell the truth.

'You are younger than me, Isaac, and not dressed well at all. No, you shall wait for me near the stables. At least I look the part; but if no reason is to be had, then we will leave empty-handed, I promise.' She glanced at his shirt, waistcoat and breeches, all once good quality, now worn to near threadbare. They fit him ill, yet they were the best he had.

He shrugged. 'Very well, but call out if you need me, sister. I will not be far away. If they spot me I will pretend to be there for the reason of asking for work. I will behave as if I came only for that and do not know you. I still think it would be better if we stayed together.'

Regan shook her head. No, she

would not risk him too; her confidence returned to her. 'Good, you head for the stable and we shall do this deed then. We will solve Mother's problems and unite our family once more.'

She hesitated just for a moment; she could tell his heart was not in her plan. Or it could have been that his head was so troubled that his heart was just aching for the return of their mother to them in her right state of mind. She paused a moment; despite all her stern thoughts and determination, perhaps it was she who needed to succumb to a moment of reflection. She stepped forward and hugged Isaac. Even though he was head and shoulders taller than her, he was still her Isaac and she had to protect him. Two years separated them, but he looked so unworldly still — at least to her inexperienced eyes.

Regan patted his back and then boldly walked out onto the lane that would lead her to the drive of the estate, whilst Isaac skirted the woodland making his way toward the stables. Regan braced herself. Everything depended on her doing this correctly, otherwise all would be lost, possibly even their mother's sanity and ultimately their access to her; and then their future would be a dismal forfeit also.

2

Regan was tired by the time she reached the large door and lifted the iron lion's head upon it. It was opened almost instantaneously, which took her by surprise. A woman carrying a pot plant and wearing an apron greeted her, looking flushed and obviously anxious to be about her own business.

'I have come here to see . . . ' Regan was ushered inside. The woman was looking around, but there was no one else there.

'Stay here, miss, please, just a moment or two. My apologies, just a . . . I shall send someone to see to thee. It's not me place to be here, oh dear . . . Just wait, please?' She was backing away, struggling to hold her burden; she almost dipped a curtsey but was hanging on to the plant so tightly that she only just managed to open a door and scurry away along a servants' corridor.

Regan's entry to the building had been simpler than she had expected, intriguingly so. It made her wonder if something was amiss in the Hall. She looked at the grand surroundings and tried to control her mingling senses of intimidation and anger. They were very different emotions that pulled her in two, but both justified by her change in circumstance and the reasons for them. How could she not be intimidated by the size of the Hall? She had been brought up in a cottage — two living rooms and a kitchen, which was considered well enough, and with its own piece of land to grow their food at the back. They even had a maid who had done for them; yet, that life of comfort was nothing in comparison to the ornate surroundings she was now experiencing. For the first time in her life she truly realised what her mother had given up to marry her father . . . or at least saw the grandeur from which she had been cast out.

'Baxter!' The sharp word jolted through the cold air inside the hundred-year-old grand building that was Marram Hall.

Regan had been staring at the decorative high ceiling, admiring the cupids looking down at her from each corner, and the crystal chandelier which hung in the centre. She had been allowed in there without even explaining why; she did not have a letter of introduction or a card to explain her arrival. A majestic fireplace opposite the doors was adorned by leaves. It had been swept clean and laid with fresh logs, but had not been lit.

Regan looked down, suddenly aware of the mud on her boots from following the path along the sheltered gill up from the coast, then the walk across fields and through woodland, and finally up the long drive. She tried to flick some of the flakes that had fallen off her as she stepped inside the immaculate and sparsely furnished square space.

Regan hoped that her dark blue military pelisse and matching bonnet would give her the air of respectability needed for her to fulfil her purpose in this loathsome place — it may as well be a mausoleum, she thought, dedicated to the lost souls who spilled their blood to pay for this family's luxury . . . She stopped her thoughts there. Her own life should have benefited also; was that not why she was here? Her father's views were deeply embedded in her soul. He followed Wilberforce's views on anti-slavery. She must think of her poor mother. Pride would have to wait until she could justify her own thoughts. Regan composed herself. She must remain calm. Otherwise, her anger would be revealed to these people and her pleas would be lost to their ears for certain.

Regan's eyes focused on the circular pattern in the marble flooring beneath her 'unworthy feet' and she smiled as, impishly, she flicked a piece of mud under the Chippendale table that rested against the wall. This family had much dirt swept underneath their hearth rugs, she mused; a little more would not be noticed. Instantly, she dismissed the thought that Mother would have been looked upon by them in the same way, which was why they had cast her so heartlessly out.

Beautiful as the furniture was, she had to admit, one person did not need so many riches whilst others did without. Her gloved fists clenched by her side. How could her family have sunk so low, that without hope of reconciliation they had been separated and disowned?

The male voice bellowed out again — nearer, louder, more persistent. 'Baxter!'

Regan jumped as she stared at the two sets of doors either side of the entrance hall, knowing that not all four led to passageways; some were merely there to give the room symmetry:

follies, possibly like this quest she had embarked upon. But she had to do something to help and there was no other plan. Momentarily she considered opening one — the one she knew would lead her to the stairs and from there to the room where the lady would be who could help her; but the voice boomed and she could not risk being too eager by being found snooping around on her own. She had to stay calm; losing her nerve now would bring disaster upon them all.

'Baxter!' The man's voice seemed more demanding than ever as the handle of the door to her right turned. Regan stood back, knocking her bonnet slightly askew as she had misjudged the wall directly behind her. Whoever Baxter was, apparently he was in for a dressing-down by the angry voice that took form only seconds after Regan's thoughts had filled her troubled mind. Perhaps this had not been a good time to present herself in such an impromptu fashion

— but desperate times called for desperate measures, and Regan was desperate.

Regan stepped forward and quickly straightened her back, facing the doorway, bracing herself as an angry yet handsome gentleman entered. In his polished riding boots, breeches and riding jacket, he cut a fine figure. Regan was taken aback by this perfectly groomed gentleman; she was expecting an angry butler or a middle-aged man, not an attractive gentleman with a strong jaw line, tousled walnut-coloured hair and striking blue-grey eyes. She took in this detail quickly as her eyes settled on the determined face of this stranger. However, on seeing Regan standing there, he seemed equally taken aback and stopped in mid-chase.

'Miss . . . ' He looked around her at the empty room, his voice much softer than it had been when summoning Baxter. 'It would appear the servants have left me for some reason best known to them. Excuse my bemusement, but I am not used to finding young maids in the entrance hall, apparently all alone. Have you no chaperone?'

Regan hesitated, but she could feel the colour of her cheeks deepen as she fought to find the correct words to say.

'Obviously not. You are . . . ?'

'I am here to see the lady of the house, sir.' Regan took a hold of her surprise and emotions and spoke with confidence . . . she hoped. She did not want to be sent away; she must find a way in to see Lady Arianne. Showing these people any form of weakness would not gain her admission. She had to act as though she had entitlement, in some way, or else she would be dismissed. Regan stood proud and held her hands in front of her, as much to steady them as to keep her elegant poise.

He closed the door behind him and walked toward her, his expression thoughtful. He looked at her in an almost intrusive way, his eyes moving up and down her body taking in every detail of her being — or so it felt to Regan, who did not care for his manner at all. Then, seemingly forgetting about Baxter, he folded his arms as he stood immediately in front of her and addressed her.

'I would believe you could be an angel who flew here on the wing, but I see you have made more earthly progress.'

'I make no claim to be an angel, and cannot see or understand the relevance of your words.'

'It came all the way from Sicily, you know, taking months to bring it safely here and at a great cost to the estate — the marble floor, that is.' He glanced pointedly down to where the speckled trail of earth led from her back to the main doors. She would normally have apologised and been beside herself with embarrassment at doing such a thoughtless thing as tracking dirt onto such beautiful flooring. However, his attitude riled her, so she stood straight, lowering her shoulders as her chin tipped ever so delicately upwards and met his eyes evenly.

'Indeed, it is ornate, if not a little lavish; perhaps it would have been more frugal to have sourced it from Derbyshire. I hear the Ashford mines are sufficient for most of our domestic needs, and provide exquisite cut designs. I feel it is always good to support local workers and manufactories.' She smiled, grateful that she had listened to her mother's tales of her earlier grander life — when she had one of her own to live, that was. Her father had talked with her of all the changes that were happening to the workforce at home as men moved off the land to find work in the vast mills and manufactories. Regan felt a tinge of guilt as she had often wondered if her mother had emblazoned her tales with nostalgia. Now she realised that, if anything, she had played them down.

'Do you? Then you must show me

your entrance hall. I fear it will be a grim place. Ashford marble is a tad dark for my taste. Besides, the Tour provided so much more than frugality for my father, who brought it back along with many other artefacts. It takes a cultured eye to appreciate the beauty and history of such things, and the wisdom of making a precious collection to be admired by future generations. However, I do not intend to stand here, in my own entrance hall, explaining or justifying the decor of my home to a total and, may I point out, uninvited stranger — young woman — who has chosen to bring her dirt into it. Pardon my being so blunt, but who in damnation are you, miss, and why on earth do you have business coming here to my front door, unannounced, unchaperoned and vastly opinionated? Those wishing to find employ within my service usually go to the rear of the house!'

'I have no intention of serving you, sir, in any way. That is not why I am here.' Regan now saw the colour deepen in his cheeks. His slightly angular jaw was set in a way that told her his patience, what he possessed of it, was fast running thin. He seemed to be a very vexed man and she thought back to the conversation she had had with Isaac about bullies. 'I am here to see Lady Arianne Coldwell, sir.' She looked straight into his angry eyes; they held hers, staring back into her own sapphire ones. Neither of them looked away for what seemed like long moments to her.

'Your card?' He held out his hand. His air of sarcasm was pointed as he exaggerated the gesture, withdrawing his hand when she did not respond and folding his arms again as if he had proved a point. Perhaps he had.

She looked at his hand, even when he withdrew it. Her pride hurt as much as her heart did, for this was not going well and her resolve was faltering. She had to remain determined and confident — but how, when faced with such

21

genuine arrogance of authority? Then she thought of her poor Isaac waiting, fretting for her, and she tilted her head upwards and met his silent challenge. 'I forgot to bring a card, sir.'

'How intriguing you are. If you know Lady Arianne, then you should certainly know of me and who I am. If you know of me then you would certainly have arranged a more respectable introduction than blustering in on the wind and bringing half of the moor road into my home with you.' He relaxed his arms. 'I must confess to being amazed by your bold manner, even though it is lacking charm. Pray tell me, where is your coach, your chaperone or your escort? Who is it that turns up unannounced and presumes to be so confidently outspoken in her opinions? I cannot believe that you are acquainted with the lady of the house. I cannot presume that you are here for any other business than to seek a position of work, but I can inform you directly that I have a full complement of staff, so your journey here has been in vain. You will have no greater success by seeking an audience with the lady of the house.'

'My name, sir, is Miss Regan . . . ' She braced herself, ready to try and win a concession to see the lady, or accept defeat. 'I am Miss Regan . . . '

The door opposite flew open and a manservant skidded to a halt as his foot lost traction on the floor as he stood on some of the dry mud. He nearly collided with Regan.

The gentleman grabbed his arm and spun him around in one strong masterly gesture. 'Baxter! Control yourself, man! What has come over this household today? I have been calling you throughout the Hall; instead you appear before me, late, as if being chased by the devil himself. Where have you been?'

'Sir, you must come with me at once. There's been an incident that needs your urgent attention.' The man glanced at Regan, his eyes taking in her appearance in obviously quick assessment or judgement of her. Baxter seemed to wish to keep his master's counsel, so she looked elsewhere, not caring to know what the distraction was, though inside she realised that fate was playing into her hands. She had made the correct decision; the brusque man would be distracted, and she would take her chance.

'Please come, sir,' Baxter added.

Regan willed him to go, to leave her, so she could make her own introductions to the lady; for it was certain this man would never let her in. He was arrogant, and she disliked his attitude. Even if his looks were appealing, his manner was certainly not.

'What incident? Has some kind of madness come over the place today?' the man queried. He turned quickly to Regan. 'You stay here! I have not finished speaking with you. I will return shortly. Do not go anywhere. I will complete my conversation with you when I return, and then I will determine what mischief, if any, you are about.' He stormed from the entrance hall with Baxter following after him, leaving her alone.

3

'Good,' Regan whispered. 'Now is my chance.' She ran at speed down the corridor, which led to the angular oak staircase and the upper landings. She remembered her mother's instructions correctly, as if she had a map etched in her mind: Regan was to take the second door to the left on the upper landing. It was there, as a child, her mother had seen Lady Arianne's younger sister-in-law Jane give birth to a son — the son who took her life's breath out of her as he entered the world.

Regan slowed slightly, realising that the gentleman must have been that same boy. If so, Lady Arianne was his aunt. Had she taken the child into her own home, and her heart, and raised him as her own? He was of the right age, perhaps six years older than Regan. The thought made her shake her head.

Of course, her mother had said he was sent away for his education; but those days were behind him now and he, apparently, had returned.

She ran on. Regan had presumed that Lady Arianne lived here alone with her servants, a lonely old woman who would welcome Regan's mother back with open arms. Now she had seen the arrogant and bad-tempered character who could be a barrier to that image of family reunion she had created in her hopeful mind. If she could persuade the old lady into seeing her way to help them, to rescue Mother from circumstance, her visit would be worthwhile. It might be that the rot in the family followed down the male blood-line, but then as she thought of Isaac, she dismissed such a notion.

By the time they dealt with whatever had flummoxed his manservant, Regan hoped that she would have gained access to the older woman's rooms and have made her proper introductions. Then all would be explained, her world would be set aright and she could tell Isaac that their life would be happy again and better than ever it had been.

Her mother had spoken well of Lady Arianne, defending her as being coerced by her husband into the devastating actions she had taken; a gentle soul who would have suffered much with conscience over the years because of their forced estrangement. Time was a great healer, and her mother had devoted years to this lady, so now was the time for that devotion to be paid back.

Regan breathed heavily as she faced the apartment's doors, taking a moment to run through her rehearsed speech. Say the most in the fewest words, she told herself. Then there would be no opportunities for misunderstandings. Calm was needed.

Regan held her trembling hand out to the door handle. *No! Calm yourself!* she silently rebuked herself, and breathed deeply to steady her mind and hand. The next few moments would change her and Isaac's lives forever — for good. She took one last deep breath and committed to her chosen action.

Opening the door slowly, she heard a woman ask the question, 'Jacobs, is that you?' The voice did not sound frail as she had expected it to; instead it was high and authoritative.

'No, Lady Arianne, it is not Jacobs. It is . . . a friend. I wish you no harm, so do not fear me. I merely need a few moments of your time to explain my situation. If I may approach, you will soon see that, although you do not know me, you knew my mother well. My name is Miss Regan . . . '

The old lady looked at her. The gentle confused air she had shown initially evaporated as her eyes focused on Regan's face as she neared her. Then her manner began to abruptly change. The woman shrieked suddenly, her voice high and piercing. Regan stopped and looked to the door. Panic filled her; the noise had been so unexpected.

'Go away! Go away!' The woman's

voice was high and charged with emotion — which one, Regan could not discern. Was it fear that was masked by the bluff of anger? 'Who is this who dares to arrive unannounced? Where is James? James! James!'

Regan had barely entered the room. Did no one want to hear her full name? Regan wondered.

'Lady Arianne . . . please, if you listen to me I shall introduce myself properly.' Regan stepped forward. She took two steps toward the woman, who was seated in a wicker window chair with a tray laid on the table to her side. 'I only need a few moments to explain to you who I am and why I am here . . . ' She took a step nearer.

Strands of the woman's greying hair escaped from her silk cap when her head shot round to face her; cold eyes focused on Regan's features. Regan felt their icy chill run through her. She could not understand why, but there was no tinge of warmth in this lady's face or manner.

Regan thought that a glint of recognition caused the lady to gasp, but the thought was short-lived. Or if it was true, the recognition did not bring out the gentle soul her mother had described — perhaps nostalgia had blurred her memory of this person. In which case Regan realised she was now in a very dangerous predicament. She had no right to be there at all.

'Go away — you are nothing to me. Horrible child — no, thief! Go away! Help me, someone!' She picked up the fruit knife from her small table and pointed it at Regan whilst frantically waving a silver bell with the other hand. 'Help me, someone! Take her away! Send me Baxter!'

'I am Regan, your cousin Olivia Harper's daughter. You remember Miss Olivia Harper? She still loves and misses you. She was innocent, Lady Arianne. You must know it. You loved her and now she desperately needs your help. Her circumstances are much changed. You can save her, milady, from the debtors' gaol. We were so happy living near York, but since Father died we had to move and things got bad. We tried staying near Whitby, but she — '

'Go, now! I will not hear this. She got what she deserved!'

'Please, just listen to me for a few moments. Please . . . we need your help, Lady Arianne, please . . . You are the only one who can give it. I know what you did, but she forgives you . . . She understood why, but your husband no longer lives, so you two can be reunited. There is no reason why it should not be so, Lady Ari — '

'Get out! You are the insolent child of a harlot, and a thief into the bargain! You say Olivia should forgive *me*!' The woman shrieked out the words, her voice breaking. 'I need no forgiveness. She deserved all she got, and more. And by God, if she still breathes, her biggest judgement is yet to come. She stole my trust. She took a heart that was not hers for the taking, and then she destroyed my life!' The woman's lips snapped shut as her venomous outburst finished.

'She could never do that!' Regan retorted, fighting back the tears that threatened to escape her. She swallowed a sob, more out of frustration and disappointment than fear. Her mother could no more break a person's heart wilfully than this lady could love with hers, of that Regan was certain. There was no help for them in coming here. Regan realised that it had been a huge mistake: time-consuming and potentially dangerous for them and her mother's situation. Now this horrible, bitter old woman knew that their mother still loved her and pined for the woman's acceptance, yet she cared nothing for Regan's mother in return or for her situation in life. Could Lady Arianne's awareness of their situation issue yet a new threat to them? Compassion was obviously not a word Lady Arianne knew, or she would not be so callous. Clearly she understood who Regan was. Her mind was clear, not blurred by time; but her conscience, if she had one, was not to be touched. Regan felt the stabbing pain of disappointment in her heart as she fought to understand how this woman's words could paint such a different picture of her mother than the one she knew so well. Her poor mother had hung on to the belief that the wicked lies that had condemned her from Arianne's own mouth had been placed there by her husband, Bertram — but no, the truth was plain to see. This woman was the wicked one; she had wanted revenge against an innocent, and she held no remorse.

'Go! Before I have James lock you up!'

'I'll go! But mark my words, you have lost your last chance for redemption, Lady!' Regan stepped boldly away, but her body was trembling with fear at what she may have unleashed upon them. The rich had power and were not to be crossed. If that man who had been so arrogant to her was anything like his aunt, he might hunt her down — and that meant Isaac, too, was in danger. Regan did not doubt that the ill-tempered James Coldwell would cross moor and dale to find them for upsetting this wicked woman.

'Evil you are, and evil shall perish! Take her!' the woman was now shouting, the fragile high-pitched voice replaced with a louder, more threatening one.

Regan wondered if the woman was in fact mad, but she had no more time to argue with Lady Arianne. She had to leave, and quickly. Perhaps Lady Arianne's delusion was down to a streak of lunacy. Perhaps it ran in the family. She hoped not. Regan heard a fluster of activity outside on the landing and quickly ran through the adjoining maidservant's room doorway; she flinched but did not stop when the fruit knife hit the wall to the right of her head. She ran back out onto the upper landing as two maids entered the room to answer their mistress's distressed calls.

Regan moved quickly to the end of the corridor, past the servants' stairwell, and hoped her mother's memory had not played her false as she followed the directions given to her. Olivia had talked of this house so many times, describing to Regan and Isaac many of its secrets. Regan pressed hard on the end oak panelling which, as her mother had said it would, released the catch on the hidden door, revealing a dark unlit flight of stairs. Here, when the house was first built, Jacobites could enter and leave unseen by all but the family through this hidden stairwell. Hunted by the government's soldiers, they found a place of shelter when needed, or a quick exit when the house was searched. The passageway had never been discovered except by the children, who explored their home and listened to the old tales of their grandfather. She closed the door behind her, her heart quickening its beat as she ignored the cobwebs and fusty smells, for it obviously had not been used in some time. Regan, now committed to her chosen folly, followed the steps down into the dark depth.

4

James Coldwell ran to the stables, his mind trying to put the image of the beautiful, arrogant wench as far from his thoughts as humanly possible. Yet he was anxious to be done with Baxter's 'incident' and return to her and see if waiting for him had improved her manners and loosened her nerve any. She seemed familiar in some way; there was something about her that struck a chord within his heart. It was strange. She had a burning anger or desire within her that he could sense, but it perplexed him as he had no understanding of it — or of her motive for pestering him on such a day. What crazed young woman would dare to present herself to him in such a fashion, and then vex him with her arrogance? He shook his head to try and rid it of her beautiful, defiant image as she even dared to criticize their taste in the flooring that her impudent feet had muddied; even questioning their right, apparently, to have it. It was proving to be a very strange day indeed.

Once he strode into the stables he found four more of his missing household servants crouching in a huddle in the end stall.

'What is the meaning of this?'

Heads shot up when his voice was heard. The staff stood back, revealing the body of a young man curled into a foetal position. The man seemed frozen in a position of agony, gripping his sides. Blood soiled his shirt. He was groaning and muttering incoherently, like a frightened child who was confused or who had had his senses pummelled.

'Who are you, man?' James asked, but could not make any sense of his muttered responses; they were not words but low groans.

'He was found in the empty stall,' Baxter explained. 'When the lad led the

Cleveland Bay in, he stirred quickly, darted for the exit and surprised the animal; it wasn't deliberate, but the animal was startled and it reared. He was crushed under its hooves. Looks like he took a bit of a pounding, he did. I calmed him down as soon as I could — the horse, that is. He is fine, fortunately, with no thanks to this ruffian though.' Baxter pointed to Isaac's curled-up body.

'Serve him right!' snapped one of the maids. 'He had no business trespassing — bet he's foreign, like. He might have come off a boat. Perhaps there's more — he could be a Frenchie. What if he's a spy?' She stared wide-eyed at James as her hand shot up to cradle her throat. 'We are always supposed to be on our guard for them, aren't we? We being so near the coast and them all across the sea.'

'Nah, he ain't French, he don't look that foreign. But he could be a horse thief,' her friend, Megan, decided.

James turned around, his colour

rising. First the young woman arrived, and now he had a trampled trespasser to deal with in his stables. The minds of his maidservants were running wild with nonsense. The day was strange indeed. 'Back to your chores, now. I will see to this, and no more wild accusations,' he ordered and dismissed the onlookers, commenting briefly on the stupidity of their speculation. 'If he were a horse thief, he would hardly fall asleep in an empty stall. Likewise, if he was a spy — what, pray, was he spying on? Or perhaps he is just a tired traveller who sought out the shelter of a stall for a few hours. He trespassed, yes, but that is all we know for now, and this is my land and I will determine what is to be done. Now be about your work and cease the gossip.'

The women quickly retreated to the Hall. He rarely spoke brusquely to them, but he rarely was so challenged by events.

Baxter shrugged. 'Megan could be right, sir. What business did he have lurking in our stables? There was no way young Seb knew he was there. Should I send for the militia?'

'No, not yet. I don't want to condemn a man before I know the truth of it.' James bent down and rolled the body over so that he could see the man's face and assess how badly he was hurt. He turned him full onto his back and tried to straighten the trembling figure. He suspected broken ribs, but no blood was in his mouth, so he hoped that the lungs were not damaged. The blood had come from a cut on his arm. His face was bruised around one cheek. Lucky, James thought, as the horse's hooves could so easily have crushed his skull.

He stared at the features before him. There was a familiarity to them, he thought for a moment, but then dismissed it as a fanciful notion. He was becoming as bad as the maids, seeing things that were not there. He was clean-shaven, but he did not have the weather-worn face of someone who was a landsman or used to helping his father out at sea. James took hold of one of the trespasser's hands and opened it up to feel the palm. His work had not been heavy. However, he was certainly not gentry either. Strange, James thought.

'Take him to the kitchens. We'll have to fetch him back to his senses before we can find out what mischief he was up to. Carry him with care, you two. Fetch water and cloth to use as a bandage. Do not injure him further. I will seek the truth from him once he is in a position to give it to me. Once we know it, then I will decide what is to be done with him.'

His groom had saddled one of his Cleveland Bays. 'Seb, when you have helped Baxter place him safely on one of the tables, you ride to Dr Abrahams and have him attend. Tell him a worker is hurt. I will explain the details as we understand them once he is here. I may know more by then.' James saw the disapproving expression upon Baxter's face.

Baxter looked up, obviously surprised. 'Sir, he could be one of the rabble; a thief who meant to harm us or steal the horse, as they said. Why would you seek to help him? Why pay for his well-being?'

'Do as I say!' James looked at his manservant and realised he had been too harsh in his rebuke. 'When I've spoken to him, or know what damage has been done, we will see; but I have no wish to see a man with broken ribs dragged to a cell by Musgrove's men, to die of internal bleeding, especially if all he did was shelter in a stable. It is possible he meant no more harm than to dent our hay whilst he slept. There were horses stabled here already, yet he did not take one. He was asleep, all alone in a dry stall. My stall. So please, Baxter, do as I say.'

'Yes, sir.' Baxter lowered his eyes, accepting his master's will if not agreeing with him, and the explanation and mild apology were acknowledged.

He turned to the stable lad, Seb, and between them they lifted Isaac's body to the kitchens. James held the reins of the Bay until Seb reappeared from the building.

'Thank you, sir.' He took hold of the reins and slid into the saddle.

'Tell the doctor that I wish him to come here and exercise his discretion. Please do not bother him with the maids' excited version of who it is that is to be seen. If this man is a local, someone will come looking for him; if not, then he can tell us his business if and when he is able to. By the time you two return I should have some answers — I hope. In haste, now, Seb!'

The lad nodded, mounted the Bay and rode back out down the drive.

James looked to the house; the wench would have to wait a while longer. He felt an inexplicable urge to return to her and explain what had happened and try to find out what her problem was. Perhaps that was it — she had come to him for help; a dispute perhaps. He sensed an air of awkwardness about her manner, as if she were there without really wanting to be. But then why ask him if she could see his aunt, of all people? It was he who was the magistrate and resided over local issues. It just did not make sense, any more than the appearance of a lad in his stall.

He shouted to one of the house-maids, Maisie, on entering the side of the building. 'Take the young lady who waits in the entrance hall into the morning room. Have her wait by the warmth of the fire, and stay with her. Ask her if she would like a hot drink, and if so, arrange it. Watch her and do not leave her on her own if you can avoid it. I will be there as soon as I am able.'

The maid nodded and ran off, whilst James stormed across the yard purpose-fully to the kitchens and to his second uninvited guest of the day.

5

Once inside the kitchen, Isaac was laid out on an old table in a cold stone-walled room. He kept his eyes tightly shut. Baxter was feeling the material of his waistcoat and checking his pockets, which held nothing but a precious few pennies, a rolled-up piece of twine, and his small knife which he used for making scrimshaw — an art he had learnt from his neighbour, an old sailor who sat and carved handles and trinkets for a living as his sailing days at sea were now behind him. He had also taught Isaac how to handle a small boat on the river. Jethro would use it to take his wares from town to town.

'At one time he must have had quality family and friends, or he is a keen thief,' Baxter remarked as he let go of his waistcoat.

'A thief who takes only well-fitting

clothes!' James commented as he entered. 'He may be growing out of them, but these were once made for him by someone with a keen skill with a needle.'

The two men stood either side of the table discussing him as if they were inspecting a laid-out corpse. Between them they stripped off his waistcoat and shirt and, with the help of Cook, wrapped his torso in wide strips of cloth as bandages to support his bruised sides. Once they had finished, he lay there, his breath seeming to heave deeply until he was rested back on the wood; but he did not cry out in pain, so perhaps the ribs were not broken.

'He could do with a good meal in his belly,' remarked Baxter. 'That's enough excuse for many to thieve their way through life.'

'Well he isn't a very successful one, if that's the only meat he has on his bones,' Cook said as she left the two men with him.

'He's pale and out of his senses. We shall wait and see what Dr Abrahams has to say when he arrives.'

James looked to the daylight beyond the doorway and his thoughts returned to his unexpected visitor. 'Dress him and keep him safe until he can be examined. Let me know when Seb returns.'

'Yes, sir,' Baxter acknowledged. 'He won't be going far.'

* * *

Isaac felt as though he was going to leap up and run away, as the effort of allowing his body to be manhandled by these strangers was intolerable; but he had swallowed back his resentment and fear. He had groaned and stayed as limp as humanly possible when everything hurt, but he did not want to betray Regan and so had acted as if he were out cold. Cold . . . yes, he wanted his 'ill-fitting' clothes back on his growing body, as they had so aptly and accurately described his condition.

Then the gentleman had appeared to him to be a good man who was prepared to help him, or at least give him a fair chance. But he needed to know what had happened to Regan before he let them see that, aside from a glancing blow which bruised, he was in fact quite healthy. So he laid there as he was re-dressed, glad now of the warmth of the extra layer of cloth under his clothes. It would keep him warmer, even if his ribs were not in need of support. So Isaac played the helpless victim. He carefully dared to peep through slightly parted lids at the stone arch of the ceiling above him. He had heard their voices, knew what they said, and tried to play to their assumptions rather than appear like a frightened child.

Isaac was ashamed that he had felt like weeping at his failings; that he had fallen asleep whilst warm and sheltered in the dry stall; for letting Regan down; and for the fate of his poor mother should they fail. He felt that he should have been man enough to make a stand, to demand what was rightfully theirs. But he also knew that if he had, he would now be languishing in an asylum as a delusional fool. Instead, he had supported his sister on her quest, knowing it to be a lost cause. If only he had stayed calm — but not as much as to fall asleep. If only he had not darted for the opening of the stall, the horse would not have reared. If only his mother still lived in such a fine house . . . If only he had his sister's courage and wisdom . . . If only . . .

★ ★ ★

Regan followed the stairs down into the dark void. Fear gripped her as the cold seemed to seep through her clothes and prick at her skin, yet she followed the path remembering what her mother had told her about where it led.

She had never doubted that her mother's words were true. For each time she told her about her life in the grand house, as she fondly called it, the details were always the same. It was not a figment of a confused mind; it was the memories of a young woman who had been greatly wronged. Now Regan knew how badly that wrong had been, because the lady who had accused her and defiled her character was bitter and twisted in her own mind. Jealousy must have been her motive, not fear of an overbearing husband, as her mother had thought.

Regan had to think carefully before she could solve this mystery, but now was not the time. She would have to meet up with Isaac again and flee; but they would return and she would confront the nephew — but not on his land, somewhere else. He must leave the estate at some point, most likely to track her down, and then she would tell him who she really was and what his aunt had done to her family. Justice would be theirs! She would no doubt be hunted now by him, so she would lure him to a place where he could not call out for his servants.

Regan calmed her mind by counting each of the steps before the corridor opened out; her spirits lifted slightly when, as she had been promised, it did. Now walking on a more level surface, she continued to stifle her fear by then counting how many paces before the end of the tunnel, and then daylight would surround her again and she would be able to push all her dark thoughts away.

Regan hoped Isaac had kept his patience and waited for her. She understood why he did not want her to take anything, though the Coldwells had so much; it was they who were the true thieves, and she and Isaac who were the victims. She pushed on the old gate that closed off the tunnel to a woodland that led eventually down to the beach. It had not been moved for some time; at first it did not budge. Regan began to panic and tried shoving the gate with the weight of her body, but it only seemed to lodge further. Tears of frustration mixed with desperation threatened to pour from her eyes. Then she thought of the arrogant face of James Coldwell and the innocent one of Isaac and she stepped back, breathed deeply and calmed herself. Brute force was not the answer. She began to pull the gate, then push. Each movement gave it greater freedom, until after some minutes it opened wide enough for her to slip through.

She had managed to scrape it free from the vines that held its secret existence for some time. This was not what she would choose to do in her best dress, but needs must. It was with a huge sigh of relief that Regan stood straight as she stepped out into the light that lit a narrow path before her. Now to find Isaac!

6

James returned to the Hall. That woman would have to explain herself quickly. His day had started off well enough, with the simple aim of riding over to Gorebeck and visiting his friend; it was a journey he had being putting off, for dear Edgar had been trying to match-make. He wanted his sister, Alice, to marry James, but the girl was only just coming out, and although pretty enough was hardly his ideal bride. She was biddable, loved playing her pianoforte, hated riding and any activity outside of their home, yet would make an excellent hostess. His aunt approved, his friend was excited at the prospect, and the girl looked at him hopefully, but James could not stand being invited to stay there anymore, for he simply felt trapped. Instead of being able to court her he felt as though he were some elder brother who was chaperoning her. She still had the mind of a child, wanting trinkets and gestures, planning her next outfit and swooning at him should he just look her way. Not at all like the wench who had blatantly stared him out in his own home. He did not care for dances and the game of matching and catching; he wanted someone with spirit who could be at his side as he took this neglected estate into the future. It could be the centre of the community in the land he loved. What use were silk slippers and frippery when there was so much to be seen and done outside?

James was taken aback; why on earth should he be thinking such thoughts now, when he was a happy bachelor — wasn't he? He had money and time and plans. Why would he want to saddle himself with a wife and children?

Since he awoke on what had been a beautiful day, determined to put an end to the nonsense of such an ill-matched arrangement in as charming a manner as he could, all had gone awry. His home was being pestered by unwanted strangers. His servants' heads were filled with nonsense about French spies, and his peace had left him. He climbed the half dozen stone stairs to the entrance of his home two at a time, expecting to see her waiting patiently for him in the room with one of his curious maids watching over her. No doubt her expression would be arrogant, determined; and yet he had sensed it had merely masked her fear. But as he swung the heavy door open, marched across his entrance hall and made his way to the room — an empty room — he stared around him, one question filling his mind: Where had they gone? Where was Maisie?

He called for her and a flummoxed young maid appeared. 'Where is the lady who you were sent to watch?' he demanded.

'Sir, she'd gone. There was no one here.'

James dismissed the girl and then

ambled back to the main door. He looked back along the drive, across the open field to the woodland, but could not see any trace of her. He shook his head. Well one less problem to bother with, he supposed, and was surprised that within his thoughts there was a touch of disappointment. He had found her an attractive distraction, a puzzle, and momentarily he had forgotten all about his need to break intentions off from Alice before someone made an inference or announcement of a betrothal on his behalf. James remembered his university friend, Armitage, who had been trapped when his engagement had been announced officially in the *Times* before he had had the chance to state he was not going to propose. He was fond of the girl, and so did not have the heart to embarrass her and discredit his own name by withdrawing.

The injured young man was enough to deal with for now. He did not see how he could be a horse thief — more a man in desperate circumstance. He was a pretty poor thief of any kind if he fell asleep on the job. James would have the truth of it and, if there were a connection between these two young people, he would know of it. James had no belief in such coincidences. He made his way upstairs.

Alice would have to wait for tomorrow. There would be no riding for him today, so he may as well change and wait for the doctor to arrive. It was as he reached the top landing that one of his aunt's personal maids, Jacobs, ran over to him.

'Oh, sir, you had better come straight away. Milady has had such a turn. She is claiming that some woman entered her bed-chamber and threatened her. She is making no sense at all; I think she has been dreaming — nodded off in her chair, perhaps. There was no one there, sir. Millie said she was downstairs and no one left. For sure, she either dreamt it or she is seeing a ghost! There was talk, sir, that one walks the halls here — from them Jacobite days ... I never seen her ... *it*, but you hear things creak when the house is dark, like footsteps and — '

'I do not approve of fanciful stories and flights of the imagination, scaring the younger servants like the impressionable Millie.'

'No, sir.' She looked and then followed him as he made his way to his aunt's rooms.

James saw a flake of mud on the carpet and clenched his fists tightly. 'This is no ghost!' He swung the door wide and entered, seeing his fragile aunt start as he entered her rooms. 'Tell me now, what happened here, Aunt?' His eyes scanned the room, but there was nothing disturbed except the lady seated in her favoured window chair, where she could watch anyone come or simply watch the sheep that wandered freely onto their land from the moor.

'Oh, James, she was here. That horrid creature entered my room and would have attacked me had I not cried out for help. Where were you? She had the nerve to tell me I would never find peace and that I was evil! You have no idea how horrid the words were that tripped off her tongue. Look — my precious fruit knife, a gift from my own grandmother, cast on the floor.' She sobbed and raised her hands to her mouth.

James saw it on the floor near the adjoining servants' room door. If the woman had used it to threaten his aunt, he thought that it was a strange place for it to be left. 'What did she want, Aunt?' James asked, and looked around the room. He bent down and picked up the discarded fruit knife. As he stood straight again he saw an indent in the wall at his shoulder height. The tip of the knife had a dent in it. He guessed that this had been thrown, and not by the wench, with its precious mother-of-pearl engraved handle still intact. He placed it back on the tray by her side. She stroked it with a shaking finger as if it was the most precious thing in the world. 'Jacobs, fetch some warm cocoa for her to drink. Have the servants search the house for a young woman in a military-style blue dress; if they see her, apprehend her. I would question her myself!'

'Yes, sir.' Jacobs left.

He pulled a stool over and sat next to Arianne's chair. 'Now, tell me what you know of her and why she should arrive here asking to see you, if all she wanted to do was throw insult in your face.'

The older woman still stroked her knife, fingering the slight dent in its point. 'She was deranged, James! Cast her into the asylum — she speaks false words and attacks me!' She waved her aged hand in the air, as if fending off further questions from him. 'You see the damage done to this?'

'Are you sure that was done by her hand?' he asked. She avoided his direct question. 'When I saw her in the entrance she seemed quite in control of her mind. It was the woman in blue, was it not?' he asked. 'I do not think it was she who threw this precious knife at you, was it?'

'You saw her and you let her up here to me! Did you know that she would abuse me so? Was that your intention? Am I to be held as a whipping boy for any harpy's amusement?' Her head shot up and she stared at him, defiance written on her face. Now she had the old fire in her belly and it was, as usual, directed at him. He ignored her outrageous outburst as he had learnt to over the years. James had long since given up hope that she might ever see the good in him or be grateful for her home and the freedom he afforded her.

'Did you know her? How?' he asked. She sniffed. Her outburst had failed again to rile him, and so she returned to staring aimlessly out of the window, looking along the drive, but did not answer him. When anger failed, icy silence usually ensued. The servants would have a bad time with her before she was abed that night. He almost felt sorry for them.

'Aunt?' he persisted. His eyes looked to the carpet to tell him more than his aunt was apparently willing to.

'She is nothing to me — nor was the harlot who begat her!' She straightened her back. She realised that she had said too much, apparently giving away that there was indeed something between these two.

'Who is she?' James stood up, but his aunt shook her head, only glancing at him fleetingly, and set her mouth in a firm line before returning to staring out of the window once more.

'She is nothing to me — and when you find her, whip her off the estate! That is what my Bertram would have done. She'll not have a penny from me, and do not let her take you in with a sob story of manufactured lies. Now see if you can find her and then send me Jacobs. I want my sleeping draft, not some hot foreign beverage!'

James backed away. 'You will have

your hot cocoa; you will not have laudanum — do you think they grow it on the moorland of Yorkshire? Do you not realise how 'foreign' the plant it comes from is? Or would that offend your addiction, my dear Aunt? It is not an answer to your problems — not that you really have any other than your ill will not to have a life you could enjoy in Harrogate. You would rather wallow and make misery here, where you could have joy and a new life.'

'You'd like that — pack me off to a place miles away and then have this place to yourself. Well I won't go! I want my draft!' She balled her hands into fists as they rested on her lap, like a petulant child.

'It is something that will quell your wits and confuse your mind. Tempting though it may be to give in to your request, I am telling you now that you will not take it in my home. Now, Aunt, I would know who this hapless woman is and what there is that is so grievous between you two, so that I may treat both of you fairly.'

'No! It is none of your concern. You do not 'treat me' at all. The place was mine, and my husband owned this Hall for years before you. You are only his heir because he forgot to write me into his will, and so it fell to you . . . a male heir. He made an oversight, that is all, and it cost me dear. You are indeed fortunate.'

James walked over to the door to her servant's chamber and saw flecks of the tell-tale mud. The visitor had very thoughtfully left a trail for him to follow. He ignored his aunt's remonstrations because he had heard them so often before. It was not, he suspected, an oversight, but a determined and final way of putting her in her place — from his grave. He was the male heir; he had kindly allowed her the freedom to come and go, to have friends visit, arrange any social event she wanted, and had even gone to the expense of buying her a small carriage so that she could go wherever she willed and whenever. Her money was her own to spend. Yet still the woman bemoaned the fact her husband had not left all to her. Perhaps because he had realised she would sell all, leave the tenants homeless and have taken rooms in Harrogate or York. The riches would be hers, but she would secrete them all and not care for the estate and its workers. To her husband Bertram the land represented responsibility to develop and sustain their wealth, definitely, but also those who depended upon it for their homes and livelihoods. James had even offered his aunt the chance to buy an apartment of her own with servants — but no; instead she clung to the Hall as if, once out, she would never be allowed back in. The thought of that pleased him, although he would never ban her when he could happily avoid her for weeks on end if he chose to. It was her who imprisoned herself.

He passed Jacobs on the upper landing as she returned with the drink on a tray. A small bottle was placed alongside it, almost hidden in a napkin. He took it off her.

'I have forbidden her this. It is no good for her.'

'Sorry, sir, but she insisted and said that she would dismiss me without references if I didn't fetch it for her when she demanded it,' she replied quietly, and swallowed as she looked up at him.

He put the bottle in his pocket and replied quietly, 'Tell her that I said I would dismiss you if you did, and remind her that it is I who pay your wages. However, take a step back when you do.' He winked at her but she did not smile in return.

'Yes, sir.' With a pale face, she quickened her step. He watched her enter the room and heard the voice of his aunt rise — and then a smash of what he presumed was the cup and contents landing on the floor. Ignoring her latest tantrum, he stood at the top of the stairs and was about to descend, but he was puzzled; the woman's almost discernible trail had gone cold. Instinct told him to look further, and he was duly rewarded. The trail, faint as it was, led to a solid oak panel. The wench had turned into a ghost, it appeared, or else she was a ghost with knowledge of his home's history. If his aunt would not explain the woman's connection to her, then he would make the attractively arrogant wench herself reveal all. No one entered his home unannounced and had the gall to threaten his aunt, no matter what her temperament was like: she was frail and old. He wondered, though, what could have driven such a fresh-faced miss to do just that. Knowing his aunt, he was not beyond believing that some of the right of it — whatever 'it' was — could be on the side of the young woman. He knew all his tenants well enough, and she was of no connection to them; of that he was sure.

He pushed on the end panel, which moved freely. It had never been sealed up, but it had been lost to history as it ceased to have been used. He would have expected it to be stiff. However, looking at the ground he could see it had been recently moved, as the dust and dirt had already been disturbed. The troubled times of yesteryear had long gone, except for the troubles abroad and the possible fear of invasion from the French. Jacobites were no more — trouble always lingers but the enemy changes, he mused, as he stared within. In which case a secret passage may one day be needed again — but he hoped not. Yet the intriguing woman knew of it. How so? His aunt would not tell him, of that he was certain. Whatever skeletons lurked in her family closet were there to stay, unless he dug them out. He tolerated his aunt because she had her own rooms in the place, her authority was limited to a few staff, and her own bitterness made her life a trial — not his treatment of her. Deep in him there was a slight nugget of pity because she had once been the lady of the Hall, and now she lived off his goodwill unless she did choose to take rooms elsewhere, as he had so frequently offered her.

James began making his way down the narrow staircase and, as the panel was pulled back into position, he realised that the pretty young wench who dared to stare back at him, with no little hint of arrogance, was a brave young woman indeed to venture down this passage in the darkness. She had courage and daring; but what menace she was upon, he swore he would find out. This was his home, and he would know what happened within it and why.

7

Isaac waited till all was silent. He had heard Baxter move to the door and open it. A chill breeze wafted over him, telling him the door had been left slightly ajar. He could no longer smell the man's musk as the air freshened around him. Isaac had listened as Baxter paced back and forth a few times, his footsteps resounding on the stone floor; something was unsettling him. He had even prodded Isaac to try and get a reaction from him. Isaac let his body stay limp and did not respond. It was a strange feeling because fear, he had reasoned, usually made one tense. Isaac was so scared of being discovered as a fraud that he fought this natural impulse and flopped like a rag doll, letting every muscle in his body relax. Then the noise of footsteps retreated and this time did not return. Isaac could feel a colder, stronger blast of air and realised the door was now wide open, for the air was saltier as it brushed over his lips and ruffled his hair. He dared to open his eyes slightly and, as he suspected, found he had been left all alone.

He was on his feet in an instant. He hobbled over to the side of the doorway, feeling the stiffness from his hip at the earlier contact with the horse's hoof, and peered out. Isaac held his nerve as he watched a laundry maid struggling with her heavy load across the cobblestone yard. When the moment was clear, Isaac ran as fast as his feet would take him to the side of the stables, slipping into the woods beyond.

He would have to find the place where Regan had told him she would meet him. If all was well, she would come out of the Hall and look for him in an open manner; if not, and things had turned bad for him, she would be nowhere to be seen. Regan had given him strict instructions that unless she was forcibly ejected from the Hall, they would have to meet in the cover of the woods and make their way back to the coast and seek a passage back to Whitby in Jethro's coble, which would be lined up with others along the coast. He swallowed; he would be going back to what made him feel so sad and desperate. How would they survive much longer and be able to free their mother? His side ached, but he knew it only to be a bruise. He had missed the full force of the horse's hoof, which was fortunate. But would they now look for him? Would he bring a search party down on Regan too? He thought about meeting her, telling her to go a different way and stay away from him; but a young woman on her own would never be safe. They were, it seemed, doomed by his inability to stay awake. Isaac ran as far and as fast as he could. He was light of foot but heavy of heart.

★　★　★

Regan fought through the overgrown shrubbery to reach the slightly broader path that led down to the coastal towns and the sweeping bay beyond. It was near here that she had shown Isaac a small hidden clearing that she considered safe enough as a meeting place. She paused and looked for any sign of Isaac coming down the wooded path. There was none. She rested on a fallen tree stump and waited, anger pushing away dim thoughts that had filled her mind since realising that the horrid woman had lied all along, and yet Arianne lived in luxury whilst their mother was trapped in a hapless situation from which she could not escape without their help. But how to help her when Regan herself had failed so abysmally?

She was lost in her own thoughts when she finally heard the sound of twigs breaking behind her. Her spirits lifted, as together they could solve the problem and make all well again. She felt it — she knew it. The future would be brighter.

'Isaac,' she said, and in her eagerness to see him Regan ran towards him. She stumbled into the open, stopped and tried to turn, to take flight once she saw her mistake. Standing before her was the handsome figure of James Coldwell. She could feel her breath quickening. Regan tried to turn on the path and make a bolt back to where she had just come from. If she could only get behind the iron gates, even though it would lead her back towards the house, perhaps once she was on his land again she might find Isaac and escape by the moor road instead; together they just might be able to flee long enough for Coldwell to lose her trail. It was a desperate thought with no substance to it at all. Where was Isaac? Could her plans go any worse than they had? It seemed to Regan in that panic-filled moment that she was destined to fail, and the Coldwells would win again. Nothing seemed to work out for her family, not since their father had died.

But their poor mother was depending

upon them. She blinked her watery eyes and stumbled. The arms that encircled her waist, preventing her from falling to the ground, yet pinning her arms to her sides, were not those of Isaac, but a much stronger and more mature male. She glanced over her shoulder and almost cried out in desperation and frustration as she realised she was clamped in the grip of the arrogant man. She could not outrun him or cast him off. She felt like screaming aloud as the injustice was so great. How could they have so much — the Coldwells — and her, Isaac and Mother so little?

'Stand still, woman!'

'Let me go, you brute! You people do not know when to stop taking and hurting people!' Regan wriggled, trying to loosen his persistent grip.

'You have lost, lady. Whatever you are about and whatever nonsense you shout, you are now lost. You will explain to me what it is you think you are doing running loose on my land, threatening my aunt and making such unfounded claims with your waspish tongue.' His voice held none of the sharp anger it had shown when he was shouting for his man Baxter, but it was determined.

'And if I do as you say, will you listen to me when your mind has already condemned me, or will you give me a fair hearing?' Her words were almost spat out as she continued to struggle in vain to set herself free of him. His grip did not hurt but held her fast.

'Be still!' he snapped back. 'You will settle yourself — and I always listen to both sides of a case, miss.'

Regan was full of fear and outrage, and the last thing she felt like doing was relaxing in the arms of this man. He was as guilty as the old woman who had brought her mother low. She would be free of the lot of them. It was too late to admit that she had been wrong and should have listened to Isaac. He had been against them 'begging' and had wanted to find a way of earning the money themselves. Regan feared that Isaac was being led astray by the well-meaning Jethro — but look what her solution had brought them. She was trapped, and Isaac . . . where was he?

★　★　★

Baxter returned to the store-room relieved, until he stared at the empty table before him. He then stormed through to the kitchens and found Cook. 'Has the doctor arrived already?' he snapped. 'I did not see his horse or Seb in the yard.'

'No! Well not that I know of, but then I spend me days in here and not in the house like you do, so why would the likes of me know who comes and goes unless they need feeding?' She continued measuring out her flour without looking up at him.

'Who moved the lad then?' He was looking around him as if expecting Isaac to appear in a corner.

'As far as I'm aware no one has come or gone from here. Are you telling me that he just up and left with broken ribs an' all?' Cook now lifted her sight to look into Baxter's seething eyes.

Baxter was staring back at her, his exasperation and anger almost palpable, but Cook just raised a questioning eyebrow. 'He has gone!' Baxter's words exploded from his mouth.

'Hmm, I thought not,' she said calmly, and began to beat some eggs. 'I suspect he has pulled the wool over your eyes right proper, Mr Baxter. The lad got a bruising but his bones are still intact.'

'Damnation! I only left him a minute to take a piss, and the lying bastard has taken flight. I'll catch him. His ribs *will* need fixing when I get my hands on him. I'll get Coombes to track him down. He'll rue the day he tried to outwit me! I'll have him in irons, you see if I don't, the lying b . . . ' He stormed out of the kitchen, cursing and no doubt denying his own stupidity.

Millie, the undercook, spoke out, 'Isn't Mr Coombes helping Mr Latham's gamekeeper to catch the gang who have been stealing his sheep over Gorebeck way?'

Cook looked up and grinned. 'Aye, he is. But if Mr Baxter could lower himself to talk to us kindly like for a change, then he might just have found that out. Now, once he has exhausted himself looking for the gamekeeper, who is not there, he will have to ask the master who will tell him where Coombes is, and then Mr Coldwell will discover that Baxter left his charge alone to escape. The doctor will arrive for no reason and the lad will be well away from it all. He only fell asleep in a sheltered stall, after all. Nearly got pummelled in the process for his crime, if sleeping can be called one! Bet the poor sod was exhausted. He looked like he needed a good dinner. If he had wanted to steal a horse, Millie, he wouldn't have nodded off, would he? Makes no sense. No, it is time Mr Baxter learned a lesson in humility.' She paused a moment, looked at Millie thoughtfully, lifted a rolling pin, pointed it at the girl, and waved it at her. 'Don't let that tongue of yours repeat my words in his hearing, or I'll take you to task and tell them you've been seeing young Seb on the quiet. Then both of you will lose your jobs. So no tittle-tattle!'

The girl gasped. 'No, I wouldn't — and we haven't . . . not like that, I mean . . . We are just friends.'

Cook laughed. 'Aye, just don't be too friendly! Now go peel those apples before they grow into trees.'

8

'Stop struggling!' James shook Regan, lifting her so that her feet were above the ground. She began kicking out, trying to make contact with his shins with the heel of her boot. Her senses were losing focus as panic overwhelmed her. She was like a trapped animal trying anything to break free.

'Put me down!' she demanded, still trying to lash out as best she could. It was with an unceremonious gesture that he did her bidding, almost throwing her into a heap onto the damp ferns that covered the woodland floor. She landed with a squeal.

'You, sir, are no gentleman!' she protested as she scrambled to her feet, frantically brushing leaves and mud from her best dress. She stepped back away from him whilst keeping her eyes focussed on his.

'Coming from a minx who fights like a wildcat, I do not take your judgement harshly. I know what I am, miss, but pray tell me what and who you are?'

'I tried explaining who I am but no one will listen!' Regan snapped as she tried to discreetly wipe a tear from her cheek.

'You know you are in a great deal of trouble. I am the local magistrate, and right now I can think of at least three charges for which I would happily have you incarcerated in the local lock-up. Before you knew it you would be in York awaiting the next assizes. So speak to me clearly — and make it the truth, because I have enough happening here today without having to deal with an arrogant young wench who attacks old ladies in the sanctuary of their own chambers.'

'Attack? Me?' She placed her hands firmly upon her hips, her temper squashing her momentary feelings of despair, and stepped forward to face him. Then, pointing in the direction of the Hall, she snapped out her reply. 'Lady Arianne is no lady, sir! She lied and spat venom at me when I sought her help. She would see an innocent woman — my mother — fall and not lift a hand to help her. Despite all that has gone between them in the past, she denies her the only help she can give to save her — us — from further shame. It is she to whom you should direct your questions. Lady Arianne caused the near-ruin of my mother once in her lifetime, and now seeks to seal her fate a second time. It is so unjust — and you spout your words about justice to me!'

Regan stepped back. Her arms dropped to her sides. Despite her temper and the desire to be strong, her emotional outburst had all but over-whelmed her. She bit her bottom lip as a wave of exhaustion swept through her body and she trembled. Regan was not a weak person, but was not used to shouting and ranting or arguing with strangers; certainly not a gentleman of rank. She breathed deeply, struggling to regain some of her normal composure. She would not give in to them. Defiantly, through moist eyes, she stared at the man who held a name she had grown to despise — Coldwell. 'It was not I who attacked. She threw a knife at me and lied, sir. You wanted the truth of it; now you have it. Lady Arianne has a case to answer.'

'So, there is bad blood between you two.' He considered her a moment. 'Calm yourself down. I will not have you making such accusations here, like a street harpy shouting them out in a public place. Whatever the truth of this affair, you will not besmirch my family name in public. I will listen to you, but first you will obey me. However, I pride myself on being just. You will return with me to the Hall. I will hear your plea and speak to my aunt. Only then I will consider what the right of it is.' He stepped toward her, then looked at her in amazement as she let out a loud cry.

'No!'

Before the man could say a word, or turn to see his attacker, he fell to the ground.

Regan crouched over him and felt his forehead. Isaac was standing over her, holding part of a branch in his hand. 'Come quickly, Regan. We must run before we are caught. I have brought trouble upon us, and they will be already looking for me.' He cast the branch aside.

'Isaac, what have you done?' she asked as she stared at James's stunned body lying on the earth, motionless. Fortunately there was no blood to be seen, but as she felt his head with her trembling hand she could discern that he had a bump already forming under his hair.

'I have saved you from a stay at the assizes, sister! I heard his threats. I know what he would do to you. This man could throw us in gaol and toss away the key. Then what would happen to Mother?' Isaac said defiantly, staring at Regan. 'We must make haste. The small boat will be there, and Jethro will have stayed with it as he promised. He is a good friend and I do not want him implicated in any part of our folly. We will take you back to Whitby. Once there I will have to make myself scarce, Regan. You see Mother. I will find work — somehow. Perhaps Jethro can guide me; he knows where a quick coin can be turned. He told me so; he knew this notion of yours would bring forth only trouble. The rich stay rich because they crave wealth and will not share it.'

'No, Isaac, you must not sell your soul to the trade. You are too honest to work with smugglers.'

'Regan, I — we — have nothing left to sell. I will pay Mother's debts any way I can. I followed you here and your plan has failed. Now mine will succeed. I have rescued you.' Isaac grabbed hold of her arm and pulled her up to her feet.

'No, Isaac, you have not rescued me. For certain, you have condemned us both and Mother to a terrible fate. If you break the law further it will make matters worse. James Coldwell was going to listen to our case. He would have helped me — us.'

'No, Regan, you do not understand the mind of such men. He would have taken you back there to his aunt and believed her word over yours. You would have been at his mercy, and there would have been no way out for any of us. We waste time here. You must follow my lead. Come — now!'

Isaac took hold of her hand and pulled her away from James's prone body. She glanced back, looking for any movement or sign of life, but Isaac increased his pace and they were soon running along the path toward the bay. Regan did not look back again. There was no time; little point. She felt as though she had come so near to finding help, only to see her hopes fall like a rock from a cliff. Now they were all doomed.

9

Isaac and Regan ran out of the shelter of the wooded gill to the edge of the beach. Locals were busy working at the daily chores: women mending nets or gathering flithers with younger children at their side; men landing their catch or preparing to set out to sea again, or heading for a much-needed drink in the inn on the beach.

The siblings slowed their pace as they made their way to where Isaac and Jethro had tethered the boat. They knew they stood out as strangers, but did not want to raise suspicion as to what they were about. So they smiled at people, talked calmly to each other and approached the empty boat.

'Where is he?' asked Regan. Panic made her voice tremble. 'I should go back and explain to Mr Coldwell before it is too late, whilst you get away. He will be angry, but I think he will listen to me.' Regan looked at Isaac's face and knew her words had failed to convince him.

'No, Regan, he will not! Jethro will be in the inn. I will fetch him. You climb into the boat and stay low. We will soon be away from this place. It has brought nothing but hardship to our mother and now to us. They thought I was trying to steal a horse. I was already wanted, and now I will be more than ever.' Isaac was standing square in front of her, like an impenetrable wall. She could hardly cause a scene here.

'Oh, Isaac, you could have explained . . . ' She had lost her argument; he did not want to listen to her any more. Regan knew that his goodwill was spent and now he had chosen a far darker path, one that appeared to have no turning back.

'Stay and hide here. I will fetch Jethro and then we will leave. We should never have come here. I will not hear another word of dispute from you,

Regan. You were wrong! We are desperate, and desperate people resort to what they have to do to survive. I will not let my mother rot in prison or my sister become a street wench!' He shook his head and stormed off.

Regan's fists clenched. She had never heard him speak in such terms to her. She so wanted to defy him. She sat in the boat debating what to do. Isaac's last comment had struck her hard. How could he think she would ever . . . ? She was frightened in a way that was almost paralysing. Never had she felt so defeated; and yet the strange and arrogant man, James Coldwell, had sparked a new hope in her heart. He had offered her a fair hearing, and she believed him to be genuine in his offer. Now deeper emotions filled her; concern and fear that they might have seriously injured him and left him there all alone. For what crime were they to be hunted down and accused of now? She had entered his home and, he thought, attacked his aunt. Isaac had been mistaken for a horse thief and had now injured him. How much more trouble could they bring upon themselves? Perhaps, she thought, if she made her way back up the pathway and told him that he had been attacked by a stranger, one of the smugglers maybe, then how could she explain how she had managed to run away and hide from them when she had so easily been captured by Coldwell himself?

Still, the truth must be told. Regan would not let Isaac throw his future away by ferrying contraband. She stood up, ready to make a run back into the woods. Coldwell would understand; he would listen to her again and realise how desperate their plight was.

She was about to climb out of the boat when she saw Jethro and Isaac running back over toward it. It was too late! Her path was blocked and her future decided. She must run like a criminal and hope that Coldwell had no stomach for a chase. Perhaps his head would be so sore he would take to his bed. Somehow, though, she doubted it. She had told him too much, and wondered if he could find them or her mother from the few facts she had given away. Her heart ached for a chance to find some solace in this visit, but she realised that the man who she had hoped would listen to her had a head that was hurting even more than her heart.

Isaac climbed in and took his seat, then grabbed the oars, followed closely by Jethro. The latter pushed the boat off, ignoring the cold water as he climbed in and took his seat nearest the bow.

Regan hugged her knees to her body, which was nestled in the small space at the stern. The boat lurched as it crashed through the breakers and into the swell of the sea. Once the men were in an easy rhythm and had pulled away from the land, Isaac shouted back to her. 'Take heart, Regan. We will free her. For now we have our liberty. Be brave, and for once in your life you listen to me!'

Regan did not reply. With the fresh sea spray on her face, her tears blended with the moisture; she hoped they would be hidden from view. Jethro was silent, his attention set upon his task of delivering his two foolish friends back to his humble cottage. Without him they would be homeless and friendless. How, she wondered, would Isaac be able to explain what he had done without losing the man's goodwill and trust?

★ ★ ★

James stirred slowly. He felt the twigs and leaves under his cheek and for a moment could not envisage where he was. With a sore head, a stiff back and dented pride, his memory returned to him. He stood up, straightened himself and squinted as he turned his face to the sky. He judged the time of day by the position of the sun in the sky above the treetops. He could not have been out cold for more than a couple of hours.

He stumbled his first few steps, then remembered the conversation with that bothersome wench — with her beautiful soulful eyes that had touched his heart. Then he cringed at the sharp pain of the blow that had struck him down. With each step he gained more balance and purpose as he stormed back up toward the edge of the woodland, where he could cross his open fields to the stables.

'Baxter!' he yelled at the distant figure of his manservant as he saw the man run from the stable block toward the gamekeeper's cottage. The fool did not hear him, so once again he was left with the man's name ringing in his ears — only this time it did, literally.

James finally attracted Baxter's attention as he crossed the open field. Sheep scattered from his path almost as if they sensed the anger and frustration that raged within him. He glanced up to his aunt's window and saw her outline; she was watching him. James would have further discussion with her once he had dragged the woman and her accomplice back to the Hall. What possible connection could there be between them? She had looked so determined, yet vulnerable. What secrets did his vexing aunt hide? He now realised that her animosity toward him might be masking other memories and actions of her apparently troubled past.

He glanced back at the woodland as a thought crossed his mind. What if this Regan had been kidnapped and was an innocent bystander in his attack? Magistrates had enemies, as the trade flourished in the area. Any man who stood up to them would be seen as an enemy to the men directly involved and the many people who sanctioned it by remaining silent and looking the other way in order to have a share in the easy coin to be made.

James had given over the use of part of his land to the coastguard service for them to use as a lookout and monitor the hoverers — ships that lingered offshore waiting for the cobles to go out and unload their goods. Illegal brandy, gin, geneva, tobacco, cards . . . the list was as long as the taxes placed upon these goods were high. The coward, whoever he was, had struck him from behind and would pay for what he had done to him; of that James was certain. If he harmed Regan, James Coldwell would show no mercy.

Baxter ran across to him, almost gasping for breath, and flushed of face. It was then that James remembered he still had another problem to deal with and a mystery to solve: who was the young man laid out in his store-room? He wondered if the doctor had arrived. His head ached where the blow had been struck, but there was no blood on his fingers when he touched the spot and he suspected no cure for a bump and his injured pride. No doubt the doctor would tell him to rest and take the laudanum he so easily prescribed for his aunt. James had seen the opium dens of London; he did not like drugs in any form. They made people hanker for them, and his aunt's character had enough flaws in it without adding an unnatural need for a liquid that would in time send her into madness.

'Has Seb returned with Dr Abrahams? James asked.

'No, sir,' Baxter gasped his reply. His eyes seemed to be scanning the edge of the woodland instead of focussing on James.

'Damn! I need my horse saddling, Baxter, and I wanted Seb and you to come with me on a mission.'

'I can't find Coombes, sir. I've being searching everywhere . . . '

'Coombes is not here today. We must search for a villain. Go back to the kitchens and tell Cook to watch over the lad. We shall have to search for the villain ourselves.' James saw Baxter hesitate and realised something else was wrong. 'Why were you not with him like I ordered?'

'He's gone, sir,' Baxter said, and

looked anxiously back at James. 'I had to answer a call of nature and the bugger just up and went. He had duped us, sir. He was not ailing like we thought he was.' Baxter stared at his master as if awaiting a good dressing-down.

The feeling of familiarity clicked into place as James thought of the face of the pretty female who had disrupted his day and resulted in his recent pain. 'I knew there was something familiar about him. They were together; there was no coincidence there. Whatever those two sought, they were here together to attain it. It must have been he who . . . ' James stopped short of admitting that he had been caught off guard by Isaac. Instead, he clenched his fists and gave an order to Baxter. 'Why could you not call a maid to watch over him whilst you saw to your 'needs'? Do I have to think for everyone around here today?'

Baxter looked away, shamefaced.

'Fetch Mr Bardwell immediately.'

James had no head for an argument or long discussion. His head was sore and he wanted to find the one who had made it so, as well as Regan. He would finish his conversation with this troubled woman. He wanted to know Arianne's secrets.

'You want the coastguard?'

'Have you a problem with your hearing now, as well as losing your ability to follow simple instructions such as 'stay with the young man'?' James glared at him.

Baxter's eyes gave away how embarrassed he felt at his failings.

'Oh, saddle my horse, man, I'll see him myself. Now please, just go!'

Baxter retreated to the stables to saddle James's favourite thoroughbred. It was a fast animal. As James collected his coat, he realised there was something he had to do before leaving. He did not want to waste any more time but he needed a name, a connection, someone to find. Once he had her, the two intruders would come to him. He entered Arianne's room.

'You let her get away!' she snapped the moment he appeared. 'I saw you stumbling back here. She will drag the name of Coldwell through the dirt she lives in unless you silence her.' The woman stood up and faced James. She was frail of frame, but her voice was strong and her heart as hard as the stone-flagged floor of the kitchens.

'Who is she?' James asked her from where he stood just inside the doorway. He did not want to waste a moment crossing the room and pleading with her to share her secrets. The time for reasoning had passed; now he just needed answers.

'She is the daughter of a liar and a — '

'No! Your accusations will not do. I asked who she is, not what you consider her to be. Tell me, or I will have Dr Abrahams declare you in need of a stay in a private institution!' He pointed to the drive, as he could see Seb and the good doctor riding down towards the

Hall. They were still distant, but they rode at speed.

Arianne gasped. 'You wouldn't!'

'Do not push me, madam. We both know I have the authority to; and the more you protest and spit your usual venom at me, the more convincing to the doctor's ears my argument will be that your wits have left you. Now for the last time, tell me — who is she?'

Arianne swallowed and stared straight back at him. 'I did not think you had a backbone in your body, but it seems I was wrong. Very well, I will say, but it will not do your name any good to be associated with her.'

She took her usual seat by the window as she watched the doctor approach. 'Her mother was my cousin, Miss Olivia Harper. She seemed such a sweet girl when we took her in, allowing her to share my home. She became my companion. When I married she was with us on honeymoon as we travelled France. That was before the troubles and wars. She returned here with us, but left the estate in shame. We covered up the scandal, but she broke my heart and trust. Olivia ran off with her lover. Yes — she wasted no time in finding another, such was the fibre of the woman. I understand that she married him — a curate. The girl was claiming to be her daughter — as if I cared. She was pleading for me to help her mother. I know not where she is, so if you have me incarcerated for my silence, it will indeed be unjust. She came begging for me to give her money, no doubt on the pretext that her mother is headed for the debtors' prison. Believe me, if that is so, then let her rot there, as she could never repay what she stole from me.' She watched out of the window.

'We will talk further when I return. Now please entertain Dr Abrahams in my absence. He has been brought here on a fool's mission.' James turned around to leave.

'Which fool?' she asked. 'Am I not to be incarcerated, then?'

'No, Aunt, you never were in danger

of that. How little you know of me — or, should I say, understand. Now I must find your cousin.'

'If you do, do not dare to bring her back into my home. You hear me . . . '

Her words faded away as James left the Hall, collecting his hat, saddle-bag, pistols and rifle. When he returned he would remind her that it was only her home if he ordained it so. He met his manservant by the mounting block.

'Shall I come also?' Baxter offered, but his eyes betrayed his reticence.

'No, Baxter, you stay here. Make Dr Abrahams welcome in the day room and send Jacobs to my aunt so that she can come down and entertain him. See if he will stay for dinner; have him use one of the rooms if he wishes to rest. Ask him to stay, and then make sure the Hall is safe — no more intruders lurking. If I do not return, have no fear; I will soon, but I am off to York and I do not know how long this business will take.'

'But, sir . . . '

'Do this!'

'Yes, sir, of course.'

James rode first to the coastguard's house upon the headland.

'What news?' Ignatius Bardwell greeted James as he rode up to his door.

'Have you seen two people leave the town by boat, horse, or on foot? One, a woman in a blue dress; the other, a young man in a waistcoat, shirt, breeches and knee-high boots.' The horse was fidgety as if it sensed its rider's agitation, but James steadied it.

'No . . . '

James sighed. 'I had hoped that from your vantage point you might have been able to pick out their trail. No matter,' James replied. He was about to kick the horse on when Bardwell spoke out.

'Not two, sir, but three; two were dressed as you say, but the older one seemed to be a sailor. Their boat headed south, toward the bay towns or Whitby. They did not look like your average group of smugglers and there were no hoverers waiting, so I thought they were just off on a journey of some sort. Was I wrong?'

'Did the woman look as though she was being abducted or forced in any way?' James almost felt hopeful that she had been, as then there would be no connection between her and his attacker.

'Not really. In fact, no, I saw her wait in the boat for the young 'un to go and fetch the elder man from the inn.'

James nodded, accepting that she was no more than a pretty lure — a distraction for whatever it was they were about. 'Thank you. Send word to the Hall that I may be away more than the one night. I will head down the coastal path awhile and see if I can determine where they have headed. I need to finish a conversation with the young lady. If, however, they return in my absence, have them kept under lock and key until I can return.'

'Very well, Mr Coldwell. Safe journey.' He nodded, but James had already gone. He had some distance to travel but, although they had a good hour's head start on him, he had a fine fast beast to cover ground in a more direct route. If as he suspected, they had headed to Robin Hood Bay or Whitby, he would soon be able to pass them on their trail. There was a mystery to unravel and a wrong to be put right. Whatever had caused them to strike him, the girl had shouted a warning to him, but he had not realised what it had been until the blow had been struck.

James would find her. She would answer his questions — she wanted to — so he would give her a chance. Miss Regan Harper was no blood relative of his, but the connection to his aunt meant there was still a family scandal that he knew nothing about. If the woman had run off with a curate, she had lowered her status, but could hardly have been called a fallen wench. A disobedient one perhaps, like her headstrong daughter. However, she must be a desperate one if she was now residing in the debtors' prison at York Castle. He would give Miss Regan another chance . . . one final one.

★   ★   ★

Regan, Isaac and Jethro rode toward the port entrance of Whitby. The ancient abbey stood proud upon the headland. Regan watched it as the swell took them first high and then low as they steered a course from open sea into the river's mouth. They had to take care, as this was a busy port: cobles and colliers went up and down the coast. They entered the River Esk and continued rowing upstream. Regan watched the red-pantiled roofs of the buildings on the steep side of the headland and cliffs, watched over by the ancient church nestled in the abbey's grounds.

Regan was relieved when the boat was finally secured and she could step out onto dry, solid land again. They had been rescued by their friend's willingness to help them: he seemed to be their only friend in the world. Regan smiled at Jethro. 'Thank you. We would have been lost without your help.'

'Yes, miss, I believe you would at that; you never mind though. My help was freely given. Your mother is a fine lady. Now, you will have to get yourself sorted out. Go to York as fast as you can; Isaac will make the money up you need to free your mother.' Jethro put his hand inside a bag he had dropped in the bottom of his boat. 'Here, take this with you now as part payment in advance, and no arguing. You take your things from my cottage in the morning and use this money to buy your coach passage back to York. Isaac will see you safely on it. It ain't much, but if you sit atop you will have some coin left to help out your ma a little, at least with food, and take a room for yourself for three nights. Then the lad will join you with more. Kip at my place tonight, for the coach does not leave until tomorrow.'

'You have already done so much, Jethro.' Regan looked at the money and realised it might have come from him helping other people to move illegal goods. It was a generous gesture; not enough to clear their mother's debt, but it would make sure she could have some decent food.

'Isaac, you sort out your women folk; leave Regan safe on the coach tomorrow, and then come back and we will talk about that work you could help me with.' He winked at her brother and Regan felt sad inside. Isaac nodded in thanks and walked towards Jethro's small cottage. Regan could not say anything in protest. Her plan to get them help had failed. For all she knew, they were being hunted, and there was no other respectable route open to her to bring help to her mother. They had to earn the money to pay off her debt somehow, or she would become ill in that place. Regan was prepared to work in a laundry if she must, but Isaac had forbidden her to find common work. He said the way to her ruin would be found in such toil. Whilst she was still young and healthy he had implied that she might yet have to find herself a suitor, but it would be a man who would be below her social position in life — or what had been her social position in life. The idea of basically selling herself into wedlock with an older man, not for love but for his needs, made her blood run cold in her veins, but she had not ruled it out. The keeper of the prison had suggested a far worse arrangement to ease her mother's plight. Whichever way she looked at their situation now, she knew they were trapped into doing something desperate just to survive.

★   ★   ★

James rode down the old Roman road — its path led straight to the ancient city of York. It was a fine, dry evening, lit by the moon and stars. He decided that he would keep riding and arrive in York late in the night. He had his rifle and his pistols on him if anyone dare to try and stop him en route.

When James approached the outskirts of the crumbling medieval walls of the ancient city, he let his horse slow to a walk. He knew the place well enough — its great cathedral; the medieval streets and narrow lanes mixed with the newer stone buildings. Miss Regan and her friend or accomplice would be making their way here to seek out her mother. The girl had said she was trapped somewhere and needed their help; trapped inside a debtors' prison. That meant she would be easy to trace and, as a magistrate, he could determine her fate.

James found a room and stabling. The evening was late, but money talked. He was a magistrate and that position gave him power. He approached the place where he had sent many a felon, be it rogue trader or fallen gentry — a debt was a debt.

This one was not his, but in these hard grey walls of York Castle, a member of his family languished.

James summoned the keeper. The hour was late and he was not at all in good humour by the disturbance, but when Master Anderson saw who his visitor was he agreed to see him.

'I tell you again, sir — we have no one by the name of Mrs Olivia Harper within these walls. Now if you will excuse me, I must insist that . . . ' The man made to close his ledger and was anxious to rid himself of James's presence; that was all too clear to see.

James stared at the portly man as he was about to close and put the ledger away, and then James realised his mistake. 'Of course you do not. Forgive me; my ride was long and may have tired my brain more than I had realised. She will have married; she married a curate. Her name would no longer be Harper; neither would Regan's. Do you have someone here by the name of Olivia?'

The man groaned and started looking down the ledger of names, starting with surnames beginning with 'A'. James looked over his shoulder and instantly dismissed ones that were too young to be Regan's mother or too old. Time passed and then they were left with only two possible matches.

'I will take you to them,' Master Anderson said in a gruff voice.

'No. You will have the one who has a grown daughter brought to me here.' James saw the man nod. He summoned his chief gaoler and the two men waited together.

After what seemed hours to James, although in truth was little more than half of one, there was a knock on the door.

'Enter!' Master Anderson shouted.

It was opened and in walked a petite woman. Her dress was grubby, yet had once been well-made. She clung to a bundle wrapped in a shawl with what, James presumed, were her few possessions wrapped carefully within it. Her eyes seemed almost too big and wide for her fine features, but there was no mistaking it: this slight woman was Regan's mother.

'Woman,' Master Anderson addressed her, 'Mr Coldwell here would like to speak with you. You will answer his questions honestly — if you have an honest bone left in your body.'

She did not acknowledge the man's words. Her eyes fixed upon James's face and he sensed her desperate, hopeful plea. She knew the name, his name, and saw in him something familiar. From her lacklustre, scared eyes a spark of hope ignited. James had come here in poor spirits, his head sore and his plans in disarray, only to find that his heart was being touched once more by a total stranger.

'Do you hear me, woman?' The keeper rapped his stick on the table in front of him and Olivia jumped as she clung to her bundled shawl.

She nodded quickly. 'Yes, sir,' she

whispered. Her voice sounded hoarse, her lips dry.

James looked at the ledger in front of him. 'You have been placed in here for a debt of £2 7s 4d owed, it is claimed, for back rent on rooms in Whitby.'

'Aye, and she owes — '

James placed four pound notes on the table. 'Her debt is now paid in full.' His attention was firmly focused on the slim figure of the weary lady who stood straight with perfect poise just like her daughter had, despite the state of her attire and her harsh surroundings. 'Tell me, Olivia, is that — ' He pointed to her bundled-up shawl. ' — all you possess, ma'am?'

Olivia swallowed. 'No, sir. They took my wedding ring, sir. It was taken off me in here along with a small silver chain. He put them in there.' She pointed to a safe that was behind the desk.

'Of course we keep certain things here for safety. I mean if they have any worth at all, they can be used to make their creature comforts better for them; but if they refuse this gesture of charity, then ultimately the items will be fairly valued and sold to the highest bidder anyway to pay off part of their debt. That is if no one comes forward to help them.' Master Anderson gave the explanation as if he were the possessor of a generous and understanding heart, but James doubted if the man had ever known the meaning of those words.

'Have they been sold yet — so soon?' James asked, and he saw the emotion well up in Olivia's eyes. 'That ring meant a lot to her.'

The keeper looked at the money on the table. James had placed his index finger upon the notes, pinning them down. 'No, sir, not yet. The lady was not agreeable to them being sold, and she has been here less than a week. I like to make sure that there is no benefactor or distant relative about to present themselves, like your good self, first before we have to look at the final options. I am a just man.'

James did not say anything. 'Give them back to her. We will disturb you no more. Make an entry in your ledger that her debt is paid in full; give me a receipt and a statement to that effect, and that she is free once more. As soon as you have completed this paperwork I will leave you to return to your duties.' James gestured to Olivia to sit on the chair by the door until all was settled.

'Thank you,' she whispered.

James poured a drink from Anderson's decanter and gave her a small glass of the port. The keeper raised his head as if to protest, but when James raised an eyebrow in challenge he looked back down to his task and his hand seemed to write all the faster. Master Anderson was keen to see the back of James and lock his money, his profit for a swift release, into the safe; that was quite clear.

Olivia sipped her drink and closed her eyes as if it were a tonic to her soul — or to hold back her emotions; James could not tell for sure. But when she opened them again, she looked at him with what he could only describe as complete gratitude.

With the officialdom done and her papers safely in James's pocket, they stepped out into the night air together without another word. Olivia looked up at the sky. She paused a moment and breathed deeply. After a few moments whilst she seemed to compose herself, she spoke more clearly. 'I knew there was good in Arianne. I knew she would help me. But where are Regan and Isaac?'

James watched her as she stared up into his face, seeking some explanation or understanding. He realised that she was sensing something was not right.

'They are coming to you, Olivia. You will see them very soon; on that I can give you my word. I have taken rooms nearby. You will please come with me and we will make you more present-able. You will need to wash, change and rest after a good meal and something to quench your thirst. I do not think they will arrive for a day or so. That will give us time to talk and know one another. You will need some new attire, and York has the finest.' He smiled at her, but her face flushed and James realised this lady had once been proud and was now in desperate need of help.

'I am so grateful to my cousin for sending you, James. I knew it was not her fault. How she must have suffered over the years with worry. Bertram's anger was a bad thing to behold. I saw a kinder side of him, but she told me of her bruises — showed me one on her arm — and I never realised what she had had to endure until then. It changed everything for all of us.' She swallowed and looked away. 'I suppose he does not know of your charitable act. I understand now how he uses his size to control her. I'm sorry for that.' Olivia looked down at the state of her dress. It was obvious that her stained clothes grieved her deeply. 'He does not know I am here?'

James was going to tell her he knew

nothing of any of this, as his uncle had been dead ten years since. But here in the street when she was taking in so many sudden changes of fortune, it was not the place to destroy her assumptions and delusions.

'I am sorry that we meet in such circumstances, James, but I am grateful that she sent you to me so quickly. That place is not fit for animals. They were so rough, and they take liberties with the inmates. They are not all bad people. I am not a bad person.'

'Come; it is cold and late and you need food, warmth and rest. Then we shall talk and you can explain what became of you, how you ended up in such circumstances, and why you were estranged for so long.' He cupped her elbow with his hand and gently walked her no more than ten minutes to an inn where he had rented two adjoining rooms. The smaller was meant for a servant and he had intended it to be for her, but on seeing this lady he could only feel aggrieved that she had had to endure a week in the cells.

She was a lady in the sense that Arianne had never been. He had known and loved his uncle well. The man was not capable of hitting a woman; so the nonsense Arianne had conjured up, and the reasons why, shocked him to the core, unless Olivia's recent stay in the prison had addled her wits and memory. He glanced at her. She had grace and gentility about her. Even now she saw the good in Arianne, a woman who would have left her to rot. James realised that instead of retrieving the bait to catch Miss Regan and her accomplice, it seemed that he had in fact genuinely rescued the mother from her fate. He presumed that Isaac was her brother, over-zealous in his protection of his sister. James could not bury the desire to even the score with him, as his head was still sore around the bump.

10

Once in their rooms, James had warm water brought up. Olivia had one dress to change into, which she had carefully wrapped within her shawl. She had saved it as long as she could. James had left her to wash and change whilst he went down and paid for fresh food and drink to also be brought up to their rooms. They were both hungry, but it was not the time to talk, for as soon as she had eaten, Olivia's eyes filled with unshed tears and then she yawned so heartily that he left her alone to sleep.

★   ★   ★

When Olivia awoke in comfort, James was nowhere to be seen. He had left her a letter, one that explained she was to receive visitors who would see that she had fresh clothes, and food would be brought to her rooms. He was going to tell Regan and Isaac the good news that she was safe and, in a few days' time, the family would reunite and a coach would take her back to the Hall. There would be time to talk and discuss the past once their affairs were sorted. She was to rest, read and wait, knowing her future was to be brighter than her past had been.

Olivia placed the letter back down and stared out of the window of her room, looking at the spires of the great cathedral. She fingered her wedding ring and silently prayed her thanks. Time was a great healer, and it was her greatest wish that the rift between her and Arianne could be sealed.

★ ★ ★

It was the next day before Regan finally made it to York. Shaken and cold from her journey sat atop the coach, she climbed down, glad that its motion had finally stopped and she was now standing on firm ground again. She was hungry and would have loved a drink of warm milk and honey — the thought almost made her swoon — but she would not spend a farthing more on herself until she had bought food for her mother.

She had taken no more than three steps in the direction of the place she hated more than any on earth, the debtors' prison, when a voice stopped her in her tracks. 'Miss Regan,' it said.

She stopped as her mind tried to figure out how it could be possible. She turned about and faced James Coldwell, large as life and standing before her. She could not tell whether it was anger, rage or some other powerful emotion that she saw in his eyes.

'We meet again,' he said.

Regan took a step backwards, looking from side to side to see if she were about to be seized by his men.

'Don't even try to run, Regan. You would not get far; I'd catch you in minutes. So where is your heavy-handed brother? Or does he only crawl around in the shadows and strike when he cannot be seen? Does he always leave you to face danger by yourself whilst the coward hides and sleeps in the stables?' He stood, arms folded, looking straight into her surprised eyes.

'You know who he is?' Regan tried to muster some confidence to face him down. She had stood up to his temper in the Hall; again she had faced him in the woods when he seemed to listen, but had been struck down. Now she was steps away from a prison, and he had the power to put her within its walls with her mother. 'You have him wrong, sir. He is honourable, brave and honest!'

James tilted his head slightly to show his doubt at her description of Isaac. 'Then does he await his time to call me out? I do not see him coming to your rescue. Perhaps he waits until I sleep in my bed and have my eyes tight shut so that he may strike me again!'

She could see how it all must look to him; but if he only knew the truth of it, he might understand. 'I need to speak with you in confidence.'

He raised an eyebrow and she swallowed.

'How did you find me so soon? How did you know I would come . . . here?' She felt light of head and yet heavy in spirits. Her world seemed to be crashing in around her, and the more she tried to stop it the worse everything became.

He came next to her, discreetly held her arm and walked her into one of the narrow alleyways that criss-crossed the city. There he stopped so they faced each other, away from the view of passers-by, with hardly any space between them. Regan was not scared of him, but of how the situation must appear if anyone stopped to look at them.

'You as good as told me where your mother would be. She owed money and was locked up. I know how the system works, Regan.'

'Please don't take your anger out upon her. Whatever I have done to annoy you, it was only to help her. She is so vulnerable; she is a lady and should never have set foot in such a place.'

James sighed. 'You see, I did not lie to you. I am a just man. I have left her in a safe place, so you have your wish. She has had her debt cleared; her attire is fresh, her body cleansed and her appetite sated. She sleeps in a comfortable bed, safe in the knowledge that you will return to her in a few days' time.'

Regan could hardly take in what she was hearing. 'You did this all for me? You know who she is and how that evil woman Arianne has wronged her?' Regan began to smile, and then she recalled the last of his words. 'Why can I not see her now?'

'Because I know little of anything to do with any of your family or your history, and I would know all. However, you are brave and you believe your actions have been for the good. Olivia is in a respectable establishment and is being tended to. I will have her well, before she is told that her idea of the truth is a myth. However, I am anxious that we talk first, especially to that heavy-handed brother of yours. He has played me for a fool, Regan, and that I am not. I am an honourable man, and I will sort out this mess you have created.'

'You said you would have her well — is she ill?' Regan ignored the jibe at her brother. This man had rescued her mother, but he was also keeping them apart.

'She just needs rest and good food.' He placed a hand on her shoulder; she felt the warmth of his touch, but although it seemed very forward and inappropriate she did not pull away. 'I want to take you to a place where you can also find warmth, wear fresh clothes, and then over a good meal you will tell me all. Then I will decide what we shall do next. Now, you tell me where that ham-fisted brother of yours is. I am sorely tempted to hunt him down and have him spend a few days inside a cell to teach him a lesson he so readily needs. I do not intend to spend my days watching over my shoulder in case he should decide to strike out again.'

Regan swallowed. 'He is not here.' She told him the truth and felt like screaming and crying at the same time. Her mother was now safe, her rescuer this man — the only man who could overrule Arianne and return them to what was rightfully their place in his family. James was a magistrate; he represented the law — and Isaac had already knocked him flat on his face. Now Isaac was definitely on the verge of committing a crime. He was joining the smugglers and would be transported if caught, or locked away in a cold, dank place where, even if he survived gaol fever, he would never be the same person again. She had already seen a great change in him. His character was beginning to harden.

'What is it?' James asked. This time his words were more softly spoken.

She looked at him, trying to decide if she dared to trust him with this latest news. However, if she did not they would never be free of the black shadow that had dogged them for what seemed an age now. It was her choice, and the price could be very high either way. Either Isaac would be saved, or he would be labelled a criminal.

'I can see fear in your eyes, yet I can tell you are not scared of me, so what is it? Where is he, Regan? What is the fool doing now?' He cupped her chin in his hand as she tried to avert her eyes, for they betrayed too much of her thoughts. He seemed to be able to read them. His own face was so close she could feel his breath on her skin. She looked straight into his eyes as if trying to fathom the level of trust she could reveal to his soul.

'Regan, trust me.' His gentle words were spoken only inches from her.

How strongly she felt his strength,

and how she wanted to wrap herself within it. To feel protected and comforted — or was it more? Could she possibly desire a man who was such a stranger to her? Isaac's words cut her thoughts. He had said he would not let her become a common woman of the streets; yet here she was facing a man, crushed together within a narrow alley, his hands on her, her mind in turmoil, her body stirring with strange, new exciting feelings. Yet she was also scared and at a loss as to what to do or say.

She pulled her head back from his palm. There was no choice, really. Regan felt that she was damned if she did and condemned if she did not tell him the truth. Resting against the wall, she looked up into his puzzled face.

'You fear for him. Tell me what he is planning, Regan, before he does something I cannot save him from. I am correct, am I not? He is seeking to release his mother, and in so doing will need funds, as you failed to turn Aunt Arianne's heart.'

'We are desperate, sir.' She blinked, not really comprehending what she was about to say. The more she studied his face, the more she seemed to fall under some kind of spell from those deep blue-grey eyes. She yearned to be able to tell him the truth and be done with it. There was definitely another far deeper yearning growing inside her. How could she be so attracted to a man whom she had only known for such a short time? To stop her thoughts, she answered him, for she did not want him to read those.

'I must have the truth. Who was the older man in the boat?'

'Isaac is not in the city, have no fear.' Regan was snapped back to reality as she realised that he already knew something about Isaac. He could easily trace him if he knew about their escape in the boat. Of course he would; there was no other way they could have escaped down coast so easily, and he had met her off the Whitby coach. She breathed in.

'Isaac is in a quandary. He feels that, as the man of our family — my father died last winter — he must sort this out. My idea for us to be restored to the home my mother was so unfairly thrown out of failed!' She snapped out the words with more force than she needed to, almost as if it were her own fault.

'Was she thrown out, or did she run away with a man — a curate?' James asked.

'My mother was rescued after being driven out of her home with hardly anything by a kindly man, who fell in love with her and brought her back to safety. He cared deeply for her, but had never met her before she was made homeless. Arianne lies. She is bitter and would see my lovely, gentle mother die in that horrid place. We have little — I was even prepared to beg Arianne on my mother's behalf — but it would have been in vain, as your aunt turned me away without giving me a chance to explain. What were we to do? My idea failed. There was nowhere else to turn. Isaac has to find work. How else were we to ever pay off the debt? He thought you were attacking me and struck out to protect me. We thought you would hunt him down. I came to tell Mother what had happened and bring her food.' Despite her best efforts, she had to wipe a tear away.

'So how is he to solve your problems then?' James asked. 'The truth!' His voice was insistent.

'I think he will be used to help carry things for some men.' She bit her lip. 'I do not know exactly what, where or for whom, but he asked for paid work.'

James sighed. 'I see. If it is illegal and he is caught, I cannot help him.'

Tears rolled down her cheeks. He wrapped an arm around her shoulders and pulled her to him. He patted her shoulder in comfort. 'You are weary and hungry. Come with me. I will take you to a place where you can find something better to wear. Then we will eat; and you, Regan — ' He wiped away a tear from her cheek. ' — will tell me all. I do not wish to distress your mother, as she is happy and content to sleep, eat and read for a few days as clothes are brought to her in her room. She will be reunited with Arianne soon enough, but for now allow her to enjoy her happiness believing that you and Isaac are only a few days away from joining her. We will need to go and find Isaac and, if he is unscathed from his adventure, I will see that he never needs to do such work again. But I will have his respect, and he will never raise a hand to me again, or I swear he will be the one who is left face-down on the floor.'

James walked Regan around the corner and along a narrow road to a medieval shop window in which were displayed clean second-hand clothes. These were either bought cheaply from fallen gentry or were cast-offs, perhaps given to servants who sold them on to make some extra coin. 'You will find what you need in here.'

He waited patiently until she came out of a narrow changing room wearing a green dress and matching pelisse. He nodded and smiled his appreciation, as he obviously thought she had good taste. He paid for her new outfit without any quibbles over the price, and Regan was surprised when she saw he had more purchases within a travel bag.

'I am very grateful for your kindness. I wish I could repay you . . . ' she said quietly to him.

He shook his head, dismissing her comment, and they left in silence. He did not say anything else to her until they were sitting eating a warm meal.

11

'You need to rest after such a meal, especially when it would appear to have been a while since your last substantial one. Do you wish to stay here whilst I return to Whitby and seek out this Jethro and your Isaac?'

Regan placed her spoon down on the empty pewter plate and shook her head. 'No, I must go with you, or how else will he know to trust you? This time he must listen to you and realise that I was correct to go to the Hall — our plea has now been heard. There must be no more mistakes, for I cannot bear it if he is in any sort of trouble. This nightmare must end here.' She sat with her hands upon her lap to stop them trembling. Fate had been playing games with them of late.

He placed his hand over hers as if to steady them as her eyes threatened to well up with unshed tears. 'Very well, you make a good point. I will take you there to him, but we will both rest first. Whatever business he is about, he will be involved in it now. Tomorrow morning we shall see him, and then his and your future will be secured.'

Regan looked up at him; her head was filled with words that her mouth simply would not form. She was so grateful, yet so scared that Isaac was now on the wrong side of the law. Could it be that her mother had been given her liberty only for Isaac to lose his?

James kept hold of her hand as she stood up and slipped out from between the settle and the table. He led her to the back of the inn and up a wooden staircase to a room. Without a word of explanation he placed his hand on the door and pushed. The door creaked as it opened wide. The room had a lit fire, one small rug before it upon the wooden planks of the uneven floorboards, and a chair to its side opposite one four-poster bed.

'You make yourself comfortable.' He pointed to the bed. It was draped with rich red heavy tapestry curtains. The fabric looked like it had been there for some time, but had been looked after.

Regan walked over to it and sat upon its rich cover, delighted that it so was soft. She noticed the night cabinet by the bed on which were a pitcher of water, a bowl, and a piece of drying cloth. She was enjoying the mattress beneath her body and was going to flop back onto it and let her mind float away into some much-needed sleep, when she remembered James was still there, closing the door whilst still inside the room.

He turned around and looked at her, smiling. 'We should be quite comfortable here. He slipped off his coat and then pulled off his boots. Standing there in his waistcoat, shirt and breeches he cut a fine figure, but it was a handsome figure that was too close for Regan. She had never been in a room alone with a man who was not her brother or her father. James was part of her greater family, but there was no blood tie between them. Even the connection to his aunt was distant, so his presence here was still very wrong.

He walked around to the other side of the bed and flopped back on it. 'Oh, I need this. Since your arrival, Regan, my life has been put in a spin. It has been an interesting few days since our paths crossed.' He looked at her, grinning as if he were far from displeased by her intrusion.

'What are you doing?' she asked as she jumped off the bed and stood looking at the wooden upright chair by the fire with a sense of dread.

He sighed. 'Regan, I have paid for rooms and clothing for your mother. I have also paid four pounds to have her freed from the prison; on top of this I have afforded your own provisions and this room. Although I am a man of means I have limited funds on my person, and we have yet to discover what folly your brother has committed. It is likely, though, that it will require funds to extricate him from it. Then there are the means by which we travel to Whitby that will also require coin . . . '

'So you expect me to share your bed?' Regan said, heartily disappointed that she had been so duped by the man. She had been so sure he was honourable, but was now thinking she had been as good as bought; Isaac's words echoed in her head. How could she deny this man, when her whole family's liberty had cost him so dearly? If he paid the debt, then he could have her mother returned to prison — or her, at his will or discretion.

He sighed and propped himself on his elbow, his hair falling across his brow. 'Regan, do you always wear your despair so blatantly upon your face? Cast whatever dark thoughts you are having of me from your mind. I am not a villain from some poorly written novella; I am a man who has helped your family — greatly, and I am one who is in need of a good sleep. You are a woman who is also in need of rest, and I am not paying for another room. So stand, sit, or lay on the floor if you must. I would suggest, though, that you sleep on this very comfortable bed and be ready to rise early for our next adventure to begin.' He flopped back again.

'Your word that you won't . . . '

'Good night,' he said, and rolled onto his side with his back toward her.

She stood for a few moments deciding what she should do; but the lure of the bed, its comfort, and perhaps the desire to know what it would feel like to lay down next to James were too great. She sat back down, gradually lowering her weight, then leaned back onto the softness. It felt so comfortable; but when James turned onto his back, the bed dipped and she found herself resting against him in the centre of that dip. They looked into each other's eyes and then both laughed. Regan was going to inch away from him, but he put an arm under her head and nestled her to him. 'Just sleep, Regan. The more we fidget the less rest we shall have. This bed has seen many a couple lay upon it, I fear.'

Regan flushed at the thought. They were not a couple, though. Then her mind began wondering what had happened on this very space and she was glad he could not read her thoughts. There seemed no respectable response she could give, so she stayed there, comforted by his warmth, feeling strangely at peace; and eventually she slept soundly in his arms.

★ ★ ★

When Regan awoke the next morning it was to a tickling sensation on her cheek, like a warm draught that made a strange sensation on her skin. She opened her eyes to see James's face close to her own as he blew gently on her cheek.

'Morning,' he said quietly.

She was wrapped in his arms. Regan realised she had slept with him, entwined with him, the whole night. She swallowed. 'Morning,' she whispered, but neither moved.

'You slept well?' he said.

'Very, and you?' she asked.

A smile played on his lips. 'Definitely. You are . . . '

'I am what?' she asked, but he shook his head and did not reply.

'We should arise and find out what further mess your brother has made for me to resolve.' He kissed her quickly on her cheek before slipping off the bed and recovering his boots.

Regan felt her cheek with her fingers as if in a trance. He ignored her hesitation as he pulled on his boots and continued talking. 'You see to freshening yourself. I will go downstairs and see what I can find to eat before we set off. Do you ride, Regan?'

'A little,' she replied as she stood up next to the jug and bowl. Her feelings were mixed. She would be in a great deal of trouble if anyone knew that she had stayed a night with James, but he was an enigma to her. He had seemed so driven at first, and ill-tempered when he had been shouting for his manservant; and yet he had been kindness itself to her mother and, although not quite a gentleman, he had been as good as his word to Regan.

He placed his palm on the door's handle. Only then did he turn around and face her. Normally so quick to talk, he hesitated. Regan glanced at him, as he did at her. 'Regan, I am not a fanciful man. I am used to my own company, and I do not like fanciful girls . . . '

'You think I am 'fanciful', James? And you think me a simple girl?'

He smiled and shook his head. 'No, Regan, I do not think you are either. I think you are extremely loyal and a brave woman; those qualities, mixed with your understated natural beauty, I find quite intoxicating. Believe me, they are far more appealing than any fancy notions some have. As I said, I am direct, Regan; so if you find my company disturbing, or my touch offensive, then I would have you tell me now and I swear that I will not burden you further with my attentions.'

Regan saw the colour in his cheeks deepen. He was not angry, but had laid open a vulnerable heart. 'I do not think either of you, James. I find you . . . pleasing.' Now it was Regan who blushed.

He nodded. 'Good. Then let us attend to our business, and then I think we may well spend time appealing to each other further.' He smiled, opened the door and left her.

Regan stood for a moment, just staring. Her heart felt full of hope for the first time in weeks. But as much as she longed to see her mother happy and her brother safe, she was also wanting to know James better.

12

The sun was bright, the air fresh, and the busy whaling port of Whitby was a mass of activity when James and Regan arrived. The noise, colour and bustle regenerated Regan's heart as she anticipated meeting Isaac again and the sheer joy of being able to tell him that they had all been saved. But then the reality hit her — he might not be able to just walk away from whatever promises he had made to these people. She prayed that he had not sold his soul to the devil. These earthly ones were known to be violent if they felt betrayed, and here she was travelling as bold as day back to them with a local magistrate in tow.

They entered the town by the older side, following the road down in the shadow of the mighty abbey and church of St Mary's on the headland. Here houses and shops were crowded like mountain goats that climbed up the steep sides of the higher land. They headed toward the old square, but James took them into the yard of an inn and had the horses stabled. Standing by the inn under the archway of the yard, Regan looked at the signage: the White Horse and Griffin. This was the east side of the town. Whitby was changing rapidly as newer, grander buildings were being erected the other side of the River Esk. It was a place of industry: whaling, shipping, sail-making, any trade connected with the sea.

'Where do we go from here?' James asked.

'I think you should wait in there, James. I need to find them and speak with Isaac first. If he sees you, he may think you have made me come here, or . . . well, it may go bad for him. Let me discover his circumstances first, and I will explain all to him and bring him here.' She tried to look convincingly into his perturbed face. It was strange to her that after only knowing this man for such a short time, his features had become so familiar to her.

'How will I know you will be safe with these people if I am holed up in there?' James said, his eyes scouting the crowd that bustled by them as if he expected Isaac to leap out again and strike him. The place was a warren of narrow streets and snickets — easy for someone to look on and then slip away. James was obviously not happy to let her go alone. This was a place where a woman could be whisked away and hidden very easily, and Regan knew that depending on whom Isaac was with, her plans yet again could be the fall of her.

'Please, James, trust me. It is better that he sees me first; then I can explain that there is no need to run or do anything untoward ever again.' She said the words with pure conviction and, as the joy they brought to her spread a genuine smile across her face, he seemed to relent and nodded back at her.

'Very well. But if you do not find him in a few hours I will seek you out,' he said, and entered the inn.

Regan would not listen to his protests; so once she saw him give in to her will, for once, she smiled reassuringly at him and walked off into the crowd.

It was not far to Jethro's small cottage, the back of which had a mooring onto the Esk. It was in a good location for anyone who was transporting goods or was able to slip away unnoticed. The building was single-storey and only had a few rooms, but it had offered them shelter and a place as a temporary home when theirs had been taken from them so cruelly.

She knocked on the old door and waited a few moments, but there was no reply. She knew fine well she should not; but despite her best wisdom, she had to find a clue to where he and Isaac were. Perhaps if they were out at sea then she could await their return. Her hand pressed down on the handle and the door opened. She slipped inside. The place was gloomy and there was no fire lit or lamp still warm, so she deduced Jethro had not been there for a while. Perhaps that meant he would soon return.

Despite being a bachelor who lived on his own, Jethro kept the place in good order. His tobacco and pipes were always neatly lined up, his linen folded, and nothing was left lying around. Even his old jumper was placed on a peg. The fire never over-spilled and the bucket of coal was clean, at least on the outside. He fascinated Regan with his ways; he was a man who liked to be busy. Idle hands were something he could not stand, and so he always found a task to do. Yet despite his neat ways and his appearance in his old worn jumper, his unkempt beard and his rough voice, he was a man of whom Regan was scared. Jethro exuded strength — a silent understated strength of character that matched his years at sea. Isaac trusted him and appeared to look to him like a father figure, which saddened her because she missed her own. By contrast, their father had been pious and gentle. It was his lack of drive and ambition that had left her family so vulnerable, when he succumbed to a fever. He never sought to climb the church hierarchy, never wanted earthly savings cooped up. Instead he would rather give and live a humble life. They never went without, but had not owned their home, bonds, coin or more than a few items of clothing. He had wanted to live simply as, he said, the Lord intended, but the Lord took him early and no one saw that coming.

Regan walked into the back room of the cottage. This had a stove which was slightly warm, on top of which was a kettle. By it were a table, chair and, in front of the window, what Jethro used as a work bench. Regan momentarily forgot that she had entered the man's home uninvited and paused to admire the fine pieces of scrimshaw that lay atop it. There were knife handles, inlays for pistols, and a larger decorative piece, which was still in the making. The workman's tools were lined up at the side, placed neatly in rows, each one clean to the point of being polished; the rag used for this was folded neatly at the side. He was so gifted, she thought, as she studied each intricate detail. It was only as she turned to look to see if the boat was tethered outside that she became aware of a stale smell within the room — musk, ale, and baccy.

Regan calmly faced the man who had silently entered, expecting to see Jethro standing there; so she was surprised when she stared into the grizzled face of a stranger.

'Now, my pretty. You should never touch a man's unfinished work. He'd be mighty cross, would Jethro, if he saw you pawing his pieces. You tell me where Jethro is and I won't tell him what I found you doing. Then I might let you fetch me a drink.' The man smiled, revealing his uneven baccy-stained teeth.

Regan stood straight, ready to face the arrogant man down. He was quite stocky and, although he wore a fine coat and waistcoat above his breeches, they were ill-kept and stank as much as he.

'You have me mistaken, sir. I am not the maid. I merely admired his work and I was careful not to damage anything and left it as I found it. So, if you'll excuse me, I shall leave you to wait undisturbed.' Regan had to pass him to leave. She stepped forward, but he used his girth to block her way.

'I don't think Jethro has a maid. He don't need one as he is so orderly in his ways. However, he may well have a doxy — even a fancy one with fine ways — or he may well buy one in for the night, for all I know or care. But I do know you are standing as bold as brass in his home, so you can tell me when he shall return, and then you can make me a drink!' He placed his large, chubby fists on his hips and leaned forward.

'I have no knowledge of his where-abouts and no intention of making you anything,' Regan answered, and tried to step around him.

Despite his bulk the man's actions were quick. He seized her wrist and in one swift move wrenched her arm behind her back before propelling her forward into the chair opposite.

Regan let out a short snap of a scream as she landed in an ungainly fashion against the hard wood. He grabbed a fire iron and held it up, gesturing with the index finger of his other hand that she should stay quiet.

Regan turned in the chair, her hands grabbing the side of the seat. 'Who are you that you dare treat me so?'

'I am the man you are going to tell where Jethro is, or you will be making me more than a drink. You will be making me a very happy man until he returns.' He waved the end of the iron in front of her face, before using the end of it to tip her chin up so that he could see her face clearly. It left a smudge of soot on her skin and the man smiled. She raised a hand to try and wipe the mark away, which made him openly laugh at her. 'Don't worry yourself; before we're through you will be a darn sight dirtier than that.'

'I do not think so.' James's voice made the man spin around. The latter pulled the iron back to take a swing, but it was a futile gesture as James had a pistol trained on him. 'Drop that! Or it will be you who drops!'

The man lowered his arm. 'You would not dare to shoot me. You'd hang, and the lady would be scandalised.'

'You fool. You would be dead. Don't try my patience. I assure you I would not hang.'

The man looked on, defeated as he discarded the poker.

'Regan, stand here. And you — ' He gestured to the man. ' — take a seat. You are going to answer all my questions, and I assure you I will settle for nothing less than the truth. Regan, pick that up,' he said, pointing to the iron.

'Who are you?'

'Silas Bland, sir. I own the inn opposite and saw this wench snooping in Jethro's cottage.'

'James, he kept asking me where Jethro was,' Regan spoke up, realising that something might be wrong.

'Well if she was waiting on him too, then I thought she might have had word. I expected him to . . . to pop by last night, but he did not show up.' The man shrugged. 'Look, I was not going to hurt the lass; I just thought that she might know something and I wanted to put the scares up her. I'm married with a family. I don't need to mess with young lasses that don't know better than to snoop in open daylight. This is a busy place, but not much goes unnoticed.' His demeanour had changed from one of menace to what Regan thought could be an honest account of what he was about.

'What was he popping by with?' James asked. 'The truth, if you wish to be safely returned to your family. Or I shall have the customs officers inspect your cellars, perhaps.'

The man's colour deepened. 'I run a respectable house, there's no need for that!' He sighed. 'Look, sometimes he brings a good offer — a barrel of something that is at a decent price. Last night I thought he was going to supply one, when he did not show. His cottage has had no light lit within it and his boat is not tethered yonder, so I just wanted to know if he was well or not. I'm his neighbour and we look out for each other.' He looked from Regan to James.

'Where was this barrel coming from? I mean the place.'

'I don't ask that. Best not to know. A good fee paid and no more said.'

'Can you ask around and find out if he returned to shore?' James asked.

The man stood up as the pistol was lowered. 'Yes, I can. I can hardly ask if anyone was arrested hereabouts, though.'

'No, but I can,' James replied.

Silas looked at him and nodded. 'Thought you might be able to.'

'Meet back here by mid-afternoon and tell me what you have found out, and I will do likewise. Jethro had a young man with him, goes by the name of Isaac — I want to know where he is,' James added as Silas walked toward the door.

'This Isaac, did he have shoulder-length mousy brown hair by any chance?' Silas asked as he put a hand on the doorframe, taking in a breath of fresh air as he stepped onto the threshold.

'Yes, that's him,' Regan said, stepping forward.

Silas smiled. 'Well you are in luck there. You'd best come with me, sir, miss.' He stepped out and headed directly for the inn.

13

James cupped Regan's elbow as they stepped out of the cottage. 'Thank you,' she whispered.

'Regan, you have a lot to learn about the world. If you keep blustering into people's homes with such blind faith, one day you will take a fall and no one will be there to pick you up. You are vulnerable on your own and it is not fitting for a lady to gallivant around the place without an escort. You are a lady, Regan, as was your mother; and before you ruin your own reputation I will have that rank restored to you. So please, take more care. As it is, you will have an uphill battle with the servants at the Hall, as you have already appeared at the door on your own and that brother of yours has made an enemy of my manservant.' He was speaking to her quietly, but his eyes were fixed ahead of him, not just on the back of Silas but on the inn and alleyways.

'They are your servants; surely you can tell them how to behave.'

James laughed. 'How naïve you are of the workings of a large house. You have a lot to learn before you mix in society, but it will be entertaining seeing you learn.'

Regan was about to protest, as she had no intention of being any man's puppet for his amusement, but she could not. They were about a more serious task; and besides, she knew James was correct. And she so wanted to learn, if for no other reason than she hoped he would be her chaperone, her teacher, and show her a life she had only previously dreamt about. Her mother would be so proud, and perhaps Isaac could have the education which he craved.

They approached the bend of the cobbled road now, where behind the inn they faced the land fell away into a harbour mouth. To the right it swept up to the abbey steps or forked into the road below the headland. Regan could smell herring from a smokehouse, although she could not see it.

'Stay close behind me, Regan. If this is a trick of some sort, you must escape — head straight up there to the church.' James nodded to the steps.

'Should I not go for help?' she asked.

'If you go straight there, you never know — you might just find it,' James replied and glanced at her for a moment.

She nodded as if she understood, but felt quite foolish, for she had thought he meant she was to claim sanctuary or hide.

Silas did not enter the inn. To Regan's surprise he ducked down the side of the building into a snicket that appeared to lead straight to the river. James's hand held his pistol ready. He was uneasy and Regan followed on, but glanced around behind her as they went, for fear they were being followed.

Then Silas stopped at a recess of a doorway. He opened it and stepped back for James to enter first. James shook his head. Silas shrugged, then whistled as he walked in. Once they were inside a lamp was lit, but only when all three had entered. Sitting on a chair opposite them, smiling and relaxed with a tankard at his side on a table, was Isaac. Around the table were three other men, all holding playing cards in their hands. Upon the table was a pile of coin and notes.

'Gambling!' Regan said the word out loud. The men looked around.

'What's a wench doing here?' one man remarked.

'Everyone in town'll know about us now,' his friend answered and laughed.

'Regan! What are you doing here, and why are you with him?' Isaac asked, but his eyes quickly focused again on the table, the men and the game.

'Looking for you!' she snapped back.

'Silas, his purse will be out of our league. What you bringing in gents for?'

one of the men shouted his question before laying down another card, cursing as he lost again to Isaac.

'He isn't wanting to play, don't worry about that. They are looking for Isaac here, and I am still looking for Jethro.' Silas leaned against the wall, watching on.

'Take him away, please, before he cleans us out — bleedin' cardsharp.' The three stood up. 'We'll ask around. Jethro should have been back last night.'

Isaac scooped up the money, stuffed it in his pocket, and stood. 'What are you doing here? You found me, so what do you intend to do now?' He stared arrogantly at James.

Before James could reply as frankly as Regan felt he might like to, she butted in. 'James has rescued Mother, Isaac. She is free at last!'

Isaac showed a moment's glimmer of relief before his face hardened again. 'I have the means to repay the debt, Regan. I did it, I will give it back to him, and we don't want Coldwell money!' he snapped.

'Isaac!' Regan stood next to him, not recognising this new mean streak in his nature.

'Coldwell? You are Coldwell?' Silas repeated. 'Bloody hell, what have I done? They'll skin me if they knows I brought a bloody magistrate in here.'

James patted the man's shoulder in what seemed to Regan like a friendly, almost apologetic manner. 'For the moment I am your guest, so leave that matter aside.' When he turned to face Isaac his manner was far from friendly. 'You have four pounds?' he asked.

'Her debt was just over two pounds,' Isaac replied, his manner uncertain.

'Olivia's debt was as you state, but then you have to factor in the 'extras' it took for her speedy release, which in total cost four pounds. Then there is the matter of her food, new attire and board. Add to this the cost of hiring a horse to bring your sister here, and her new attire; and then, if you have gambled sufficient to pay that off, on what will you live?' James stood before him.

'I challenge you,' Isaac blurted out.

'You what? You want me to fight a duel? I'd down you in one shot or slice you in two. Either way, your life would be cut very short. Don't be a bloody fool, man. You have neither the maturity nor skill to beat me.'

'No, not a duel. I challenge you to a hand of cards. If I win, whatever your choice of game is, all debt is clear and I can use my winnings to set us up in a cottage.' Isaac smiled and pulled a chair back from the table.

'And if you lose — what then?' James asked.

'Then you have your will. Take the lot and I become your puppet.' Isaac almost sneered and Regan could see the spark of annoyance in James's eyes.

'Isaac, there is no need for any challenge. James will take us back to the Hall where we belong; we can have a real home again. We are no longer in need of charity or help.' Regan could see these two men squaring up to each other like two fighting birds.

'I have a position to uphold . . . or is he a coward?' Isaac said, and grinned.

James's reaction was quick. He kicked over the table and stood before Isaac, pointing the pistol straight at him. Isaac backed to the wall, his eyes wide. Regan gasped, but knew in her heart that James would never shoot a man in cold blood, yet Isaac was pushing for a lesson that she had been unable, or unwilling, to deliver when his immature temper had surfaced.

'I do not sell my soul in order to make a point. I do not sneak up behind people in the woods and strike them down when they are in mid-conversation. I stand before them, call them out, and fight my battles like a man. I do not skulk in another man's stables whilst the woman goes forth. I would never desert my women folk for a game of chance. So do not direct the word 'coward' at me again, or I will

169

challenge you to a lesson in life you will not easily forget. Now tell me where Jethro is.'

Isaac was looking at the pistol's barrel. Even in the half-light, beads of sweat were visible on his brow. 'I'm not a coward. I had to make the money some way, and I always beat Jethro, so he told me where to come to play. We cannot pay you back, but I wanted to free my mother. Regan wouldn't listen to me.'

Regan saw the despair in Isaac's eyes. She stepped next to James. 'I know you meant well, but my plan did work. James listened to me.'

Isaac looked at her. 'You call him James, yet you are strangers. Don't let him dupe you, Regan. He all but owns us. He can use you because Mother's fate lies with him. He owns her debt now. Don't you see? He owns *us*.'

'What little faith you have in mankind, young man.' James lowered his pistol and turned to Silas. 'Was Jethro on a run last night? And if so, where?'

'It is worth more than my life to tell anything to you. I have a family I love dearly, and their lives I would protect at the expense of my own.'

James glanced at Isaac. 'Those are the words of a real man. Take note, Isaac, and then one day you might be one.'

Isaac's shoulders rounded and he glared at Regan.

'If I give you my word I will not act upon what you tell me in here in my official role, but I seek this man Jethro, will you tell me when he is located?' James asked one of Isaac's colleagues. 'I would know what has happened to him.'

'Why?'

'He helped these two,' James replied.

'Very well, he was supposed to be meeting a ship, a Frenchie off up the coast. They had brandy — good stuff, but he did not show and his boat has not entered the harbour.'

'Then when you know what has befallen him, send word to the Hall. He risked my wrath by helping them, and possibly saved a genteel lady's life in the process. If it is within my power, I will return the favour once — but only once. Now we must go.' He pointed at Isaac. 'You learn a lesson in humility quickly, or you and I will have a lesson taught away from anyone else!'

Reluctantly Isaac nodded. They made their way back to the inn.

14

Two days later they returned to the Hall in a coach. Baxter was irate when he saw Isaac arrive as a guest, but not as much as Lady Arianne was when she cast eyes upon Olivia, who was shown to the best guest room upstairs. James had the maids settle them in: fresh water and clothes were brought to them and a meal arranged before he would let either side meet.

Arianne burst into his room as soon as he closed the door behind him, glad to be home, excited by the prospect of knowing Regan more, and happy to have a family again to fill some of the empty space in the large Hall.

'You brought her here. She tried to steal my Bertram away from me. She would have taken him from me, and you bring her back here!' The lady was irate.

James stood, walked over to the door, which had been left wide open behind her, and closed it. 'Aunt, you do not burst into my rooms unannounced. I bring to this place those whom I choose. I believe you wronged Olivia many years ago. Fortunately she found love, which was so obviously lacking here. She has two fine children, now fine adults, and she has my promise to make amends for all that has passed. She has a kind heart, and I believe that Uncle Bertram was indeed fond of her. The shame is that you could not see beyond your own possessive jealousy that he loved her as a younger sister and nothing more. Instead you drove her away, lied about his treatment of you, and no doubt drove him to an early grave with your infernal nagging and demands! I have rooms prepared for you in Harrogate and you will spend most of your time there near your friends and associates, with two servants to do your bidding.'

'You would insult me so, and you

know so little. I will not go! I will not be driven away from my home!' Her hands were in fists as she spoke.

'No, ma'am, you will not, because this is not your home and it is time you realised that fact. This Hall belongs to me because my uncle willed it so. I have had enough of your poison. You will leave in three days' time. It is your choice if you wish to meet and seek your cousin's forgiveness. If you do not, then go and make peace with your conscience in Harrogate.' He calmly walked over to the door and opened it wide. 'Good night, Aunt.'

She turned and walked over to him. 'I will rot in hell before I will accept that woman in my life again!'

'That is your choice,' he said, and closed the door behind her.

★ ★ ★

Arianne refused to come out of her rooms at first, but curiosity and her last chance to present an icy front and an awkward air got the better of her. She did not speak, but joined them in silence at meal times, watching and saying nothing. This continued until her coach arrived. Then with one solitary word, 'Goodbye,' she left. Olivia took two steps toward the coach but Regan caught her arm, and she gave up her plea for Arianne to acknowledge her.

James left with his aunt to make sure that all was well when she arrived at her apartment. It was one he had been preparing for her for a while. He had used it himself and knew it to be in a fine location. After a cursory tour it was time for him to leave.

'If you need anything, you only have to ask. However, funds have been made available, so you have your independence, Aunt.'

'You are so like him, James.' Her voice was tired for once, as if the fight had been taken out of her.

Her words took him by surprise.

'You seek justice, seeing the good when others see the harsh reality of life.

He loved her, yes. She perhaps thought of him like a brother, but he lit up when she walked into the room. I could never kindle that spark within him. I was jealous because I knew his heart, but could never own it as she did. You see I was a good match, but she would have been his love match.' She glanced down at her gloved hands.

'Let it go, Aunt. There is tragedy in this and you have lived in the shadow of it yourself. Live again, free of it, and let me make amends to Olivia and her children.'

He saw her head look up at that last statement, and her face broke into a smile. 'How history repeats. She is like her mother and you are like my Bertram. Your eyes sparkle when you see Regan, and hers do at you. But watch that Isaac. Send him away too, for he will be lonely and jealous.'

'Don't worry, Aunt. He is going to have the choice of an education or a commission, but he will not languish there at my expense.' They exchanged smiles and a knowing nod as they parted.

'Visit,' she shouted to him as he stepped outside.

'Yes, Aunt, I will,' he replied, and left knowing he would, and realising that sometimes there is a very thin line between right and wrong.

⋆ ⋆ ⋆

The following weeks went by more quickly than James had ever known time to pass. Isaac happily agreed to be sent to a private college where his education could continue, once Jethro had been located and rescued from a lock-up in Scarborough. He too had agreed to try to turn over a new leaf.

Olivia was unsettled at first, but then a surprise visit from Arianne saw both women chatting animatedly; and much to Regan's delight they returned to Harrogate to have fittings for new wardrobes made. When James came to collect them Olivia did not wish to leave straight away, and the two cousins stayed on whilst Regan and James returned to the Hall.

'Can we ride together again, James?' Regan asked.

'Too much chatter in the parlour for you?' he asked as the coach jostled along, his mood instantly affected by her smile and company.

'They have a lifetime to catch up on, and if I have to be instructed on anything else I should do in polite society I fear I shall scream. So many rules, so much fuss over the smallest mannerism or comment.' She shook her head as she watched the countryside go by.

He laughed and she looked at him, puzzled.

'You are a delight. You are so graceful in manner, and yet you have the heart and mind of a rebel. Do you like the estate, Regan? Is it not too isolated for you?'

'Heavens, no! I am confounded by the assembly rooms. I seek no pleasure in being eyed like the latest prize. I love being outdoors. I do not like sewing, but can when I must. And I want to have purpose in my life, James.'

'Then have purpose with me.' His smile had dropped.

'You want a companion?' she asked.

'Don't tease me, woman. You know what I want.' He took hold of her hand. 'There is not room in this coach for grand gestures, but I will ask you now. Marry me, for I will look over your shortcomings in the assembly rooms and you can look over mine for not taking you to the ghastly places in the first place. Help me to develop the estate. I have such plans for a school and almshouses, and I want someone to share my vision with me.'

It was her turn to laugh. 'James, you sound as if you want a partner in a business, not a wife.'

'I want both.' He slid his hand behind her head, his fingers entwined in her hair as he pulled her close to him so he could kiss her with a growing passion that excited her as much as it took her by surprise. Regan melted into his embrace, absorbed by new sensations that overwhelmed her with delight, until the coach jostled and she landed atop him between the seats.

Their laughter only subsided when they became completely engrossed in each other's embrace. She gave him her answer as the coach rattled on along the rough tracks, taking them home.

With great will and effort they managed to sit aright again. Words were no longer needed. Regan had fallen into trouble, off a seat and into the arms of the man she loved.

THE END

CHLOE'S FRIEND
A PHOENIX RISES
ABIGAIL MOOR:
THE DARKEST DAWN
DISCOVERING ELLIE
TRUTH, LOVE AND LIES
SOPHIE'S DREAM
TERESA'S TREASURE
ROSES ARE DEAD
AUGUSTA'S CHARM
A STOLEN HEART

We do hope that you have enjoyed reading this large print book.

Did you know that all of our titles are available for purchase?

We publish a wide range of high quality large print books including:
Romances, Mysteries, Classics
General Fiction
Non Fiction and Westerns

Special interest titles available in large print are:
The Little Oxford Dictionary
Music Book, Song Book
Hymn Book, Service Book

Also available from us courtesy of Oxford University Press:
Young Readers' Dictionary
(large print edition)
Young Readers' Thesaurus
(large print edition)

For further information or a free brochure, please contact us at:
Ulverscroft Large Print Books Ltd.,
The Green, Bradgate Road, Anstey,
Leicester, LE7 7FU, England.
Tel: (00 44) 0116 236 4325
Fax: (00 44) 0116 234 0205

TAKE ME, I'M YOURS

Gael Morrison

Melissa D'Angelo is tired of being the only twenty-four-year-old virgin in Seattle. Before entering medical school, she needs a lover with no strings attached. Harvard Law School graduate Jake Mallory loves women and they love him. But a pregnancy scare with a woman he barely knew birthed a vow of celibacy and a growing need for love, family and commitment. The moment Jake and Melissa meet at a local club, passion ignites. But Melissa can't allow sex to lead to love — and love and family are all Jake wants . . .